SPLIT SCREAM

VOLUME SEVEN

OFF THE MAP

Featuring:

JOHN K. PECK / L. MAHLER

&

ÍDE HENNESSY

Content warnings are available at the end of this book. Please consult this list for any particular subject matter you may be sensitive to.

SPLIT SCREAM, Volume Seven © 2025 by Íde Hennessy, John K. Peck, L. Mahler, Alex Ebenstein

All rights reserved. No parts of this publication may be reproduced, distributed or transmitted in any form by any means, except for brief excerpts for the purpose of review, without the prior written consent of the owner. All inquiries should be addressed to tenebrouspress@gmail.com.

Published by Tenebrous Press.
Visit our website at www.tenebrouspress.com.

First Printing, March 2025.

The characters and events portrayed in this work are fictitious. Any similarity to real persons, living or dead (except for satirical purposes), is coincidental and not intended by the author.

Print ISBN: 978-1-959790-35-8
eBook ISBN: 978-1-959790-36-5

Cover illustrations by Evangeline Gallagher.

Interior illustrations by Echo Echo.

Cover and interior design by Dreadful Designs.

Edited by Alex Ebenstein.

For those feeling isolated. You're not alone.

INTRODUCTION

The novelette has been dismissed and disparaged. Some dictionaries don't even define them as a unique form, listing only short stories, novellas, or novels. Others write them off as being "too sentimental" or "trivial".

This is silly, of course, and, with little effort it's easy to see the novelette has a purpose and value.

What makes a novelette, then? Exact word counts vary, but these stories are longer than a short story and shorter than a novella. In this case, between ten and twenty thousand words; or, horror you can devour in about an hour or two.

Sound like another form of storytelling?

I'm not saying a novelette is a movie is a novelette. And I'm not saying written fiction *needs* to be like movies. But . . . But they are *kind of* like movies in terms of length and threads, right? If you're willing to accept that premise, at least for the moment, may I present to you . . .

SPLIT SCREAM
A Novelette Double Feature

Truly, what better way to present these stories than as a double feature? Do you *have* to read them back-to-back in a single Friday night after dusk? Certainly not. But could you? Absolutely.

Shall we?

This volume takes us off the map, to unnerving and isolated towns. The first is "Evergreen" by John K. Peck & L. Mahler, a nature horror in a bad-luck place, featuring a mysterious tree growing in a closet. Íde Hennessy's "Sequoia Point" follows, where a grieving widow moves to a tiny vacation village in the off-season. The lack of folks is made up for in spades by the inexplicable doubles and supernatural occurrences.

You ready? Grab some popcorn, turn the lights low, and don't be afraid to scream.

This is Volume Seven of SPLIT SCREAM, the series on year four now. A heck of a ride we're on.

Whether this is your first time with us, or you've read one of the previous six volumes—thanks for joining the ride.

Long live the novelette!

Alex Ebenstein
Tenebrous Press
Michigan, USA
December 2024

CONTENTS

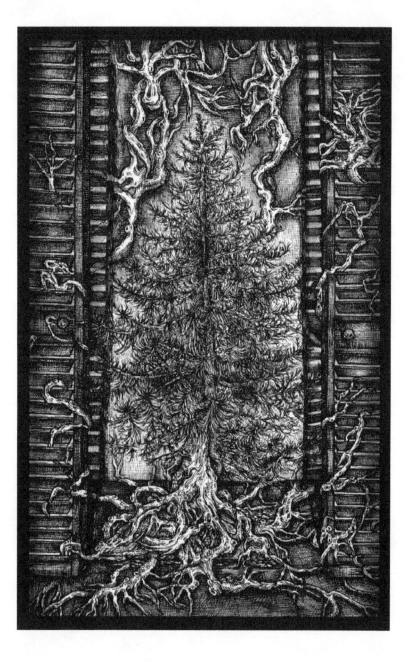

EVERGREEN

John K. Peck & L. Mahler

*T*hey wait. They listen. They peer in at the dark fringes, spread gnarled fingers to block the light where it gathers. They taste and smell and sense the throbs of life that move amongst them. Most of all they thirst, with a deep, relentless pang. They thirst for the coppery flavors of the life-throbs that meander past, unaware, otherwise absorbed. They thirst and yearn and watch, feeling the ache of proximity. And when the time comes, they feed. Joyously, in concert, fingers meshing and twining, pulling, drawing in, consuming. And in the wake of this feasting there is renewal. Delicious abundance.

The residents of Falls Valley have vanished. The town stands empty, punctuated by the snap of screen doors in the wind and the hum of flies circling half-empty plates. Stocky black letters on the single-screen cinema's marquee announce a second-run film playing to an auditorium of vacant seats. Shopping carts sit idle in the market aisles, soft music playing from the tinny speakers overhead.

Aside from the near-total silence that stretches along Main Street and pervades side streets lined with wood-frame houses, Falls Valley is unspectacular. The distant drone of the highway is a reminder of a mid-county bustle that never crept close enough to bring tourists or traffic. A dense wall of redwoods surrounds the town on all sides, and the shops along Main Street, most long-shuttered, stand dark and empty.

The morning mist has burned away, and now the sun bears down from a cloudless sky, gleaming off parked cars and window glass, creating a strip of light along the main thoroughfare. The road is bordered on both sides by squat one-story buildings, beyond which stands the shadowy bulk of the tree line. A lone figure makes her way into the gauzy darkness of the forest at the south edge of town, a dark silhouette with fists balled into the pockets of a faded denim jacket, bobbed hair swept over her face. She stares intently at her feet as she walks, unfazed by the persistent silence all around her.

Falls Valley, population 900, was one of a dozen near-identical Redwood Alley towns that hugged the Perch River, settlements built into a forest that seemed to spool out endlessly east of the highway. The river originated in the jagged line of foothills some 50 miles south of town, meandering northwards through Redwood Alley. The towns themselves punctuated a dense swath of forest that was broken only by the highway to the west. But Falls Valley was a bad-luck place, people used to say, *something in the dirt*. Deirdre had grown up there and taken a grab-bag of memories with her when she left for the city: dangling by scraped knees from the monkey bars in the park, lining up for ice cream at the deli in summer, smoking cigarettes in the field past the school auditorium. The pastoral remembrances muddied a darker undertone that she hadn't acknowledged until long after she left.

It was a place where sour-faced shopkeepers often lasted less than a year, leaving doors chained and windows blocked out by newspaper. Housefires and car accidents were a little too frequent, and misfortunes on a spectrum from lost keepsakes to grievous injury seemed rampant. Even the tap water had a bitter tinge to it, something the residents had always attributed to the stony foothills that separated the region from the rest of the state. It was a place where people came and went without much fanfare.

Like so many before her, Deirdre left as soon as she could. Content with her curated set of memories and a vague distaste for traveling anywhere north of the foothills, she had no intention of ever returning. Then, just after the new year, a call arrived.

"Deedee?" A voice not entirely unfamiliar. And the name, a moniker she'd left behind a decade prior. In the city she was Deirdre, straightforward and serious.

"Yes?" she said, with the smallest hint of annoyance.

"Deedee, it's Debra Wells, out past you on Stone Pine. I know it's been a long time, and I'm sorry to be the one to tell you this, but your mother's passed."

Fragmented thoughts crowded her head, unable to materialize until she took them one at a time. The first was her recollection of Mrs. Wells, a dim memory wrapped in goose down and grocery store perfume, foggy hints of porch-side lemonade, rides to school in a pickup truck with patched-up tires, the small, teary funeral after her youngest was presumed drowned at the swimming hole, though the body was never found. Mrs. Wells was the closest neighbor to her mother's house, to what had once been Deirdre's house. What would be her house again, she supposed. That was the second thought; others followed from there.

What struck her about the following month was not the unexpectedness of that call, nor the smooth neutrality with which she took the news, nor the dizzying speed at which she found herself standing beside a suitcase in the entryway on Stone Pine Road, surveying the house she'd once believed was her whole world. Despite it all, what stood out was the curiously administrative nature of the proceedings, and her swift efficiency when faced with the business of death. Fifteen days into February, and all that remained of her mother was a ceramic jug of ashes scheduled to be delivered the following Monday before noon.

There wasn't a funeral, nor a need for one. The few neighbors who remembered her mother hadn't much liked her, as she was a woman known for her stern nature and frequent calls to the police to complain about trespassers wandering onto her property or raccoons toppling her trash cans.

The house—*my house,* Deirdre thought, with an insistence that took her by surprise—was eerily unchanged. The stiff perfection of everything in its place: her mother's jacket hanging neatly in the corner, circular rug centered precisely beneath her feet, rain boots squared heel-first against the wall. Her mother had liked disorder even less than noise, and the house was a shrine to her particularities.

After her father left, Deirdre and her mother carried on more as roommates than family. The house, largely free of the drama that plagued a decade-long marriage of mismatched expectations and constant misfortune, settled into an uneasy calm in which Deirdre spent time in her room or outside in the yard, at friends' houses for dinner, in school or at the swimming hole depending on the season. Her mother shuttled between the master bedroom and kitchen, where she had set up a workspace framed with tidy piles of manuscripts, doing the editing work that kept them afloat. She left the house only for errands and the infrequent social obligation.

As she grew up, chafing at the staleness of the house and the smallness of the town, Deirdre began to observe her mother with a detached sense of curiosity, as one might take in the shabby nooks and corners of a doctor's waiting room. She had already begun to sense that Falls Valley was in fact her version of a waiting room. The months and years until her eventual emancipation stretched out bland and tasteless before her. The days rolled out like waves, the seasons indistinguishable, summer and winter alike marked by the spiny chill in the air that came with the altitude and ever-denser tree line.

It was during this long stretch of time between childhood and adulthood that she began to notice unfamiliar keepsakes appearing around the house. They were small, trivial items, knick-knacks of a sort, presumably brought home by her mother, which struck Deirdre as entirely out of character. She would return home in the afternoon to find a thin stack of baseball cards with folded corners on the sideboard in the hallway, or a gold-plated lighter standing on its base next to the kitchen sink. She once found a green plastic hairbrush placed beside the candles on the mantel, as if with careful intent. More objects appeared and disappeared without explanation, leaving tiny trails of mystery in their wake: a silver money clip empty of bills, a plastic compact that smelled of rose-scented hand lotion, a pocket-sized notebook with deep creases on its cover, waxy pastel crayons tied with a dirty ribbon.

Falls Valley soldiered on as it always had, residents taking in stride what had come to be half-expected, from illnesses and bankruptcies to the growing list of available properties taped up in the window of the town's sole real estate office. Eventually the realtors left, and the paper listings curled and discolored in the sun. The swimming hole was fenced off after one too many summertime tragedies. The deli owners took an extended vacation after a widespread bout of food poisoning. *A bad-luck place.*

Deirdre finished her last year of school and packed a suitcase with all she cared to keep. Her mother drove her to the bus station, and they parted with a brief embrace. *It's safer out there*, her mother had said. That was the last time Deirdre saw her, a pale figure in a station wagon, holding up her hand in a silent, frozen wave as the bus pulled away from the curb.

She lingered for a moment in the entryway, watching dust motes filter through the patchwork light of a weak afternoon sun. The house, compact despite its two stories, had a tendency to feel cave-like—corners shaded murky black even on sunny days, footstep echoes thumped a tad too loudly. After so many years in the city, she had forgotten what real silence felt like, with its cool, angular corners and big empty spaces. The urban backdrop of sirens and lives unspooling in close quarters created a silence of their own, but one that had always felt familiar, safe, a wash of miniscule distractions. This silence, in this house, *her* house, was vast and full of shadowy possibilities.

Leaving the suitcase at the door, she walked down the narrow hallway that led to the living room, where a creaky screen door opened onto a square plot of manicured yard. A wall of windows offered a view of the forest that spread outwards beyond the back fence. As always, a pair of candlesticks stood on the mantel, a thin layer of dust the only sign that her mother was indisposed. She followed the wooden staircase up to the second floor, where the two bedrooms faced each other from opposite ends of the landing. The door of her old room was ajar, as it had always been—*we don't have closed doors in this house,* her mother's voice scolded faintly, years removed—and through the opening she saw a neatly-made twin bed, a bureau with worn handles, and a bookshelf packed tightly with rows of the paperback novels she had consumed greedily as a teenager. Directly in front of the stairs, the bathroom gleamed from behind the half-open door, blue and white tiles meticulously cleaned.

She walked towards her mother's bedroom and stopped in front of the door, hand resting on the cool metal knob, eyes peering into the slivered darkness. Though the doors remained ajar in her childhood home, this had always been her mother's realm. Deirdre had a vague recollection of the room, the layout of the furniture, the dim light cast by the corner window with its view of the trees, the feel of her mother inside it. But as she entered, the smell took her by surprise: sour, yet tinged with mossy earth. She walked to the center of the room, considering the tucked-in corners of the bedspread, the sweater folded on the dresser, the curtain pinned carefully beside the window, and breathed in the smell, her mind working to find its source.

A wooden dressing table with bowed legs and bronze handles occupied the space below the window. She remembered its hunched silhouette from the rare occasions she had peered into the room as a child, recalled thinking it resembled a boxy crab frozen mid-step, perpetually hovering. Now, standing beside it, she noticed neat piles of knick-knacks. There was a sewing kit with a cardboard wrapper, a half-empty pack of chewing gum, a leathery eyeglass case, and a cowboy romance novel with worn-out corners, all stacked around a semicircle of wide candles and tidy jars filled with dark, chalky powders. She raised an eyebrow and laughed to herself. *A decade later and still a junk collector.* Yet this was not the source of the smell, which grew brighter and more pungent, deeper somehow, as if a small, dark corner of the forest had manifested itself, with its nooks and insects and mulch and damp, here inside the house.

She found herself in front of the closet, where the smell was intense enough to bring tears to her eyes. Slowly, carefully, she pulled the slatted wooden doors apart. The smell rolled out, thick and sharp in her nostrils. And there, in place of hanging clothes and ordered rows of shoes, was a form: ambiguous in the dark but nonetheless solid and real, a deeper, darker shadow in the blackness, motionless and standing at chest height. Her eyes adjusted, and she took a step backwards. Before her, rooted in the center of the closet, was a tree. A cedar by the look of it, with knotty branches that splayed outwards into fingers of evergreen fringe. Its thick trunk wound down into a neat triangle of soil, and its roots labyrinthed along the closet floor in waves and whorls, emerging from the soil and vanishing again into the spaces between the wooden floorboards.

Deirdre remained motionless, considering the tree as its smell dissipated into an odd familiarity, wondering how and when her mother had decided to plant a tree in a second-floor closet. How it had survived, seemingly content in the dark, with no trace of dampness or root damage in the living room below. Why it was here at all. She kneeled, careful to avoid the soil scattered by the closet doors, and studied the spot where the trunk met the pile of earth. There, a tiny corner of paper jutted out, the earth around it darker and damper. She extracted it between thumb and forefinger, brushing away the dirt that clung to it. In the dim bedroom light she could see that it was a business card, or a section of what had once been a business card, the tiny silhouette of a hammer and the first part of a name—*Theo Bar*—all that remained on its wrinkled upper portion. The jagged edge was stained a deep red, and it left a sticky film on her fingers, not unlike sap.

She stood there, partial business card held aloft towards the window, red sap drying on fingers, questions coursing through her mind. She stood there until the doorbell rang, a distant series of chimes that shook her back to reality. She went downstairs to find the town's police chief at her door.

"Well. Good afternoon, Deedee Towhee."

She knew the crooked smile grinning at her from beneath the olive-green service hat. Dark eyes, thick brows, a thin scar snaking across the left temple.

"Hello to you too, Milo Abara. It's been a while."

They smiled at each other from either side of the open door.

"Miles now, actually. They tend to take me more seriously that way." He gestured at the badge.

"I know what you mean. It's Deirdre for me. But you've done well for yourself since Ms. Bornim's study hall."

"Yeah, strange how things turn out. I'm sorry about your mom. I know you weren't close, but I'm sorry all the same."

"Thanks. I didn't think I'd ever be back in this place."

Deirdre looked around, at the towering trees on all sides, at the grown-up Milo standing before her, at the driveway with its haphazard cracks grown through with roots and weeds. Then he stepped forward and they hugged, and she had the sense that time had looped around, that these older versions of themselves were a mistake of some kind, that it was just last week they'd spent the night in the woods, their hands entwined in the dark, smoking cigarettes, watching the stars, and swearing they'd leave Falls Valley for good.

"I came by to see if you need anything." He paused just long enough to indicate spontaneity, then continued. "Coffee maybe? The deli's long gone, but the Sugar Pine is still hanging on, and they still have cherry pie."

"That sounds more like dessert." Deirdre raised an eyebrow and held his gaze, thinking about the unexpectedness of the past month. "But sure, let's do it."

The Sugar Pine was almost completely unchanged, a relic encased in wood veneer, grill smoke, and fluorescent lights over vinyl booths that perpetually sagged beneath the weight of phantom guests. The diner was empty, and Deirdre and Milo walked to the same booth they'd shared as teenagers, sitting across from each other. "Not much changes around here," he said, reading her expression. He paused and looked out the window. "Well, people leave or disappear. But I guess that's nothing new either."

A server in a stained apron headed towards them, tattoo curling around his forearm, hair dangling in his eyes. She recognized him as Bo Sellers, a younger kid she'd never liked, who was always either smirking or smoking, and who, worst of all, had always seemed perfectly at home in Falls Valley.

"And some people stay," she mused.

Bo pulled out a wrinkled notepad, and his smirk grew into a wry smile. "Hey, Milo. And hey, Deedee Towhee. If you couldn't get out, none of us had a chance."

The strangeness of hearing her old name twice in one afternoon brought with it a twinge of the distaste she still felt for people and places ten years removed.

"I'm in town on family business, not staying I'm afraid."

"Surprised you cared enough to come back for that."

Deirdre stiffened, wishing she could close her eyes and wake up to sirens and street noise, to being Deirdre again. Milo, ever the diplomat, made small talk, ordered pie and coffee, and smiled at her in a way that both apologized and commiserated.

"I still have it, you know," he said, once they were halfway through their pie.

"What's that?"

"The book you gave me that night, in the woods. Before you left. *The Stranger*. We had it for senior year English, but I never read it, and you couldn't believe it. I read it after you left. You were right."

"I'd forgotten," she laughed. "What was I right about?"

"The way he describes being alone. That it's all he wants, but the noise of people and obligation always gets in the way. I liked it." Milo grinned.

"I'm glad," she said.

They sat over coffee until the sun went down. A scattering of regulars came in for dinner. Deirdre insisted on paying, and as they left she grabbed the pen Bo had left behind with the receipt and put it in her back pocket. It was impulsive, childish even, but as they sat and talked about a decade gone by, as she tried to ignore the server's sideways smirk, the blank faces of customers coming and going, the dark fringe of the tree line casting ever-longer shadows outside, she had begun to think that she never stopped hating this place and the people in it. That Milo had made a mistake staying here, that they both should have left just the way they'd planned that night in the woods. Stealing the pen was a silly gesture, but a gesture all the same. After all, Falls Valley was a bad-luck place.

They sense. They feel. Roots plunged deep, arms spread skyward, they feel in waves, pushes and pulls, sensing change as a shift in wind. A new one, they whisper, a young one, in the language they favor. Low and coarse, soft soil rolling over itself. Their knowledge of time is other, meted and measured in eons, but they sense that the waiting is sharper now, jagged with anticipation. The new one cannot hear them yet. But it will. *Of this they are certain, a surety beyond certainty. In the meantime, they bide, they push and pull with deep, slow breaths. They pace in ways the life-throbs cannot comprehend.*

Back at the house, Deirdre sat on the bed in her mother's former room. She stared at the outline of the tree, the shadows of its roots stretching towards some unknown destination. She hadn't told Milo about it. At the Sugar Pine, under the sickly white of the fluorescent lights, it hadn't seemed entirely real. But sitting in the dark, smelling the sharp tang of earth and sap, sensing the outline of branches brushing against the closet walls, she thought that the tree made some kind of sense.

The forest played only a minor part in her childhood, despite its proximity. Falls Valley was built into a ridge, its streets flattened from hillocks and stands of pine and cedar, its houses forced out of plots rampant with muddy stumps and fallen needles. Root systems yanked from earth, wild branches and tangles of foliage replaced with orderly single-family homes, weekly trash pickups, gravel roads, and irrigation pipes. Living in Falls Valley meant pretending that the dark shadow of the forest didn't really exist, that the town would keep the trees out, cubicled into allowable spaces. The forest was a presence, looming and somber, but always on the periphery. She, like nearly everyone else in town, had never fully acknowledged it, had wandered cursorily into its edges and driven on the few roads that cut through it, but never trekked deep into its heart.

But the forest encroached in fits and starts, saplings burrowing through roadways in the spring, tangled roots snaking under fences and through flowerbeds. In the city, she never found herself missing or even thinking much about the forest; there were trees and even a few urban forests in parks and at the city's outer edges, but she never noticed them. They faded into the background with the smooth, synthetic feel of a built environment, just another part of the scenery. Here the trees felt different, and not just because of their omnipresence. They were somehow denser, greener, *realer* than trees elsewhere.

Since her return, she'd felt the forest as much as seen it, sensing its presence, expectant and infinitely patient, wherever she went. Standing outside a storefront on Main Street or stepping from the curb in front of her house, she could swear she felt something like a branch brushing the back of her neck, or a pulse underfoot like a root pressing through pavement. When she looked up at the treetops, they would occasionally seem to shudder despite the lack of breeze, quivering palpably before returning to stillness, and she would avert her eyes, troubled, and continue on her way.

She fell back on the bed, staring up at the ceiling, her vision moving from where the tops of the white-painted walls met the unpainted wood-panel ceiling, across it to where the light fixture hung on its metal chain. As a child she would lie in her room on her back and imagine the ceiling as a floor, imagine herself stepping over the strange high-threshold doorways, lying down against the sloped surfaces that led upward to the walls. *Get off the floor and clean yourself up,* her mother's voice from years past, memories of reluctantly rising from the coiled cotton rug, feeling the blood rush to her head as the world returned to a dull and disappointing regularity.

Don't fall asleep here. It wasn't as much a voice of reason or responsibility as one that sprung from some deeper unknown place, causing her to sit upright so quickly that she became lightheaded. *Like a damn kid.* After a moment the swimminess in her head receded, and she stood, leaning against the bed to get her footing. She told herself she should cross the hallway to her old room and go to bed, but she couldn't stop staring at the black void of the open closet in front of her. As her eyes adjusted, she stared beyond the two slatted doors, folding outwards as if reaching for an embrace, until the room around her faded. She could just make out the outline of the tree, blue-black against a deeper darkness.

Hands on her hips, she slid her fingers into her back pocket and pulled out the pen. She held it up, reading the rounded '70s-looking logo, *Sugar Pine Diner,* and pressed the button at the top of the pen. The tip came out but immediately sank back in. She tried it several times, but it refused to click into place. *Christ, even the junk here is cursed.* Then a flash in her mind, the image of the business card fragment protruding from the dirt. She stepped to the threshold of the closet, leaned down, and pushed the pen tip-first into the soft dirt at the base of the tree, deep enough that all but *Diner* was covered. *Contain the mess,* she thought unevenly. She brushed the dirt off her hands, then walked to her own room, leaving the door ajar on her way out.

She woke quickly, snapping her eyes open as if she'd heard a sound. For a moment she wondered where she was, how she'd ended up someplace so quiet, where the sirens and car engines and shouts of the city had gone. Once the scene settled into place, she let herself relax again, breathing in deeply, noting the mossy scent of old linen, and below and beyond it, an even fainter scent, vaguely acrid, like fresh soil mixed with rust. She remembered traces of a dream in which she'd been walking through the halls of a massive institution, looking for someone to let her out, doors closing and locking behind her in an increasingly claustrophobic cycle, until by the end she was trapped in a single room.

She rose from bed and moved absently through the various steps of a morning routine, as if watching her past self carry out each action with the requisite familiarities intact: stepping high and carefully into the tub; balancing against the dresser as she put on her socks; giving the refrigerator handle a harder-than-normal yank to open. She felt both out of place and at home in each room, and moved through them with an unexpected agility.

Outside, the freshness of the air was startling. A late-morning mist persisted, unwilling to give way to the brightening sun. The disparate combination cast a bluish light on the streets and buildings, bathing the trees at the edge of town in a deep-hued coloration she couldn't recall seeing before. On foot, she found herself back at the Sugar Pine, though she hadn't intended to return, at least not so soon after her last visit. But with more empty than open businesses in town and a caffeine headache creeping its way between her ears, coffee had become an urgent necessity. She entered the near-empty diner, sat at the counter, and ordered eggs and toast with coffee. From behind her, the door chime tinkled brightly, and she turned to find Milo with his service hat in his hands.

"Couldn't stay away?" He walked towards her and placed his hat on the counter. Ten years gone by, and much to her surprise, his smile was still able to put her at ease.

"No," she said, "guess not. And I needed some coffee."

Milo nodded, his eyes remaining on her. "I'm here most mornings. It's pretty much the center of town.

Everyone passes through here on their way in or out." He paused as a server approached. "Isn't that right, Laney?"

"Must be the coffee." Laney winked and handed him a to-go cup.

"Got you working mornings too now?"

The woman shook her head as she wiped down the counter. "Kid didn't show up, so I'm on a double."

"Sorry to hear that," said Milo, before turning back to Deirdre. "I wanted to ask, if you're not busy tonight, maybe we could get dinner"—he lowered his voice—"at a real restaurant, no offense to this lovely spot. There's a place in Deventer called the Railway that's pretty good. My treat this time."

She flushed, pausing just long enough for a hint of doubt to flicker in his eyes. "Of course, yes."

He nodded slightly, and she mused at how right it felt, how familiar she'd let herself become with his presence despite her animosity for the town and everyone else in it. "So, small-town police chief, you must work, what, dawn to midnight? Cracking cases, bringing down multistate conspiracies?"

"Actually, *Deirdre,* I'm off at six tonight. So I'll pick you up at seven."

She laughed and replied, "It's a date."

"Okay, then," he said, turning and half-shouting a farewell to Laney before stepping out the door into the brightening day.

The Railway turned out to be nicer than expected. *Romantic even*, Deirdre thought. The walls and ceiling were made of wide redwood beams, and the crocheted runners and burl candle holders stopped just shy of being hunter's-lodge kitsch.

They ordered a bottle of red wine, and Deirdre was enjoying the warm lightheadedness it brought as she emptied her second glass. *Slow down, at least wait for the food to arrive.* But something about leaving Falls Valley had made her feel both more awake and more relaxed, as if a weight was lifted from her shoulders. She held her glass, rotated the wine in slow, red swirls, and watched Milo as he recapped everything she'd missed in the last ten-odd years. A few deaths, mostly older people, but also a couple of teenagers she vaguely knew as kids, whose car had sped off the road north of town a few years before. Some feuds and breakups, and fewer weddings. Apparently they'd filmed a few episodes of a TV series in town, but it was canceled before it ever aired. *Fitting,* she thought. *Should've filmed in Deventer.*

And of course, there had been the disappearances. "The problem," said Milo, "is that it's not rare for people to just up and leave without telling anyone. If we hadn't been close before you left"—he stared directly into her eyes as he said it, and she felt herself flush for the second time that day—"I would've had no idea whether you left or disappeared. So without a direct police report, we have to give it a week or so before we can start an investigation. Of course some are reported, but people have learned there's not much we can do." His brow furrowed, and he fidgeted absently with the table runner. "You might think we're a clueless backwoods department, but it's an impossible situation. It's like people are just here one day, gone the next."

Deirdre considered reaching across the table to touch his hand, but their food arrived, and she instead took a small, quick sip of her wine before setting it back on the table.

As they ate, the conversation went further back to their days at Redwood High School, to shared memories of the rumors, fights, rivalries, and occasional friendships and romances that had marked their teenage years. Milo recounted a dare to camp at the graveyard on the edge of town, spooked boys huddled in a damp tent in the dark, drinking coconut rum filched from a liquor cabinet and listening to warbling folk songs on the only radio station that could penetrate the surrounding hills. She considered her own stories, buried deep but still fragile, with ragged edges that resisted prodding. She smiled as he recalled run-ins with hapless security guards, classes cut to hitchhike down Redwood Alley, driving into town with the headlights off at night to watch the stars streak past in a cloudless sky. Her own stories stayed buried, sharp edges safely out of reach.

After the plates were cleared, Milo leaned towards her, his voice hushed. "By the way, Jeanette Lund is still around. I'd always expected her to head out the day after graduation, but she's still here, still in the same house. She had a baby a little while ago, but nobody knows who with. And her grandma died recently, so she's there alone with the baby, but yeah—weird how things work out."

Deirdre's chest tightened. *Jeanette.* Why had Milo suddenly brought her up? Deirdre thought back to her junior year, when Jeanette and her friends had been seniors and made her life hell, or at least made her hate school and herself and pretty much everything. *Heard your mom's got the cops on speed dial.* Always something petty, nothing offensive enough to warrant a slap or punch, but right at the edge. *Gonna wear those shoes to the dance? I left those at Goodwill last year, thought I'd never see 'em again.* Jeanette always delivered her cutting remarks with a lopsided wink, and as Deirdre seethed, struggling to think of a response, Jeanette and her friends would walk away, their laughter echoing in the linoleum-floored hallways. Now the best she could manage in response was to look straight ahead and give a raised-eyebrow *huh*. An awkward silence followed, broken only when the bill arrived.

On the way back to Falls Valley, the headlights pooled around the gnarled tree trunks that framed the roadway, and they slid back into an easy silence. She felt warm and comfortable, watching Milo's hands on the steering wheel, his eyes on the road. She put a hand on his knee and he turned to her, smiling. Then, in an instant, the lights went out. Her heart beat loud and fast, eyes snapping wildly from side to side, striving to make out familiar shapes.

"What's happening?" she shouted, fingers scrambling across the dashboard, blood pulsing in her ears.

Then Milo's voice, calm and smooth: "It's just the headlights. So we can see the stars."

Her eyes adjusted and took in the straight stretch of roadway spooling out in front of them, the darkness like liquid spilling through the car windows. The stars were an afterthought, but the trees pushed in, fingers outstretched, breathing in the darkness. She thought she could hear them, a low thrum, barely audible beneath the hum of the engine. *Dee. Dee. Dee. Dee.*

"Please, Milo," she whispered, "turn the lights back on."

They exult. They surge. They sense regeneration, taste it deep in their cores, the nearness of growth a cold gasp, guzzled greedily from within. The tallest of them reach beyond the peaks, above the mist, limbs hardened by searing sunlight. Their great torsos gnarl and soar, seemingly still but thrumming with strength. The tallest of them have keepsakes of their own, nestled in joints, lodged in rough crags and cracks. Here a cold, glimmering oval on a delicate chain, there a circle with glossy face and hands that long ago ceased to move. Remnants of regeneration, tokens rising as years wither away. They rejoice with each sliver of what remains.

She paced the living room, studying the two new candles in their holder, their unburnt wicks jutting upward at odd angles. Milo had walked her to the door but hadn't lingered, and after a quick hug he'd headed back to the car and driven off towards downtown. Her mind jumped from Jeanette to the low, coarse sound of the trees filling her ears, then back to Jeanette. Her uneven wink and pointy smile. Hair flipped over her shoulder as she walked away, trailing laughter. Deirdre had chosen to leave Falls Valley, and there was a strength in that choice that had sustained her through the past decade. But in returning, that strength had retracted into a compact little ball. She hated the way the town made her feel, and she hated herself for letting it get to her.

She walked to the kitchen and ran the tap, leaning down to drink directly from the faucet like she'd done as a teenager. *Would it kill you to use a glass*, the walls seemed to echo. She turned off the sink, wiped her mouth, and felt her pulse slow, her anger recede. She went upstairs, undressed, brushed her teeth, and got straight into bed, clicking off the nightstand light and plunging the room into blue darkness.

Eyes closed, she thought back to dinner, about the warmth she'd felt drinking wine and listening to Milo talk, how his dark eyes held her gaze until she looked away, a warm flush in her chest. She thought about the drive home through the forest, back up the straight stretch of highway that linked Falls Valley to Deventer, before it twisted north past a half-dozen increasingly tiny forest towns. She thought of the slippery darkness when he turned off the headlights, the black branches of blacker trees heaving towards her, beckoning her, quaking with the judder of the car engine.

Then she opened her eyes in the darkness. What was the thing Jeanette had said that day in the locker room, while Deirdre shivered in a towel, still dripping from the shower? *Deeeeedee,* they'd always start, emphasizing the first syllable in a mock-yearning voice, *DEE-dee, you better hope you fill out soon, you're gonna be flat as a board when you graduate. DEE-dee, nobody's ever gonna want you, why don't you just leave town already.* Her pulse quickened, and her eyes burned. Jeanette was snoring away a quarter mile down the road, in that ugly little green house at the far end of Quarry Lane. She remembered walking by it late at night, wishing she had the strength to throw a rock through the window but never quite mustering the courage. She hated that the one time she'd met Jeanette's grandmother she seemed friendly enough, wondered what had happened to make her granddaughter so small and nasty. Mostly, she hated that she could still picture the house, knew the route from her own house by heart. She lay on her back a few minutes longer, then turned the light on, got dressed quickly, and slipped outside into the night.

The small neighborhood at the western edge of town had always been a lackluster blend of tree-filled vacant lots, single-story houses, and small light-industrial shops, but now it seemed that the streets had become even grimier, with weeds growing in the sidewalks and trash scattered in the gutters. The buildings had shifted and settled unevenly, their brick and plaster exteriors run though with cracks, dark windows like gaping mouths in blank faces.

Jeanette's house was the last building on Quarry Lane, with only a small open lot between it and the street's dead end. It was much as she'd remembered it, but smaller somehow, dirtier and more run down, its green paint faded to a drab olive-gray. The stone walkway to the front door was lined by dead grass on both sides, short and trampled into a flat, shiny surface that reflected the moonlight. The front porch was concrete, elevated to the height of a single step, with just enough space for a worn-looking white plastic chair.

Deirdre approached the house as quietly as she could. At the door, she noticed a small wreath, about the size of a salad plate, hanging just under a diamond-shaped window. It was made of plastic, with waxy ivy leaves and bursts of red flowers. Without thinking, she reached out, pulled it from the door, and ran back to the street.

She kept a brisk pace all the way home, and by the time she reached the front door she was breathing heavily, heart racing with something more than exertion: excitement, or more precisely, anticipation. She took the stairs two at a time and walked across her mother's room to the closet, pulled open the closet doors, and kneeled, breathing in the strange, sharp scent.

She turned the wreath over in her hands. *Even the junk here is cursed.* A deep breath, the smell pouring into her, filling her throat and lungs, mellowing into a sap-tinged aftertaste not unlike whiskey. *Dee. Dee. Dee. Dee.* The sound of the trees crept in through the window, their echoes filling the space around her, until the air pressed against her like a thick blanket. Were they speaking to her, really? She closed her eyes, breathed the smell, felt the wreath's spiny plastic leaves under her fingertips.

"Deedee."

Her eyes snapped open. *Not in your head*, she thought. *You heard that, out loud.* But the room was quiet, empty, only the darkness, the tree, and herself, kneeling on the faded floorboards, wreath in her hands. She glanced at the tree's base and the soil beneath it, and there, ever so gently, the dirt had been pushed aside, making way for a thin coil of root. She reached out to touch it, tracing its knotty contours. Softly, she caressed the length of the delicate spiral and held her breath, swearing it had responded to her touch, a slight push against her outstretched fingers, a loosening of the coil. Gently, she moved the root aside, then pushed the wreath into the gap in the dirt. Her fingers came away damp and slightly red, and when she brought them to her nose the smell of sap and tannin was almost overpowering. She walked to the bathroom and washed her hands until the reddish-umber color disappeared and the water ran clear.

There, staring at her hands against the shiny ceramic sink, she thought: *But what happened to the pen? The pen is gone. Bo is gone. Bo's gone the way of the pen.*

The moon was higher in the sky by the time she made it back to Jeanette's house, and the dead lawn out front was almost reflecting it in full. She crept past the house and into the vacant lot beyond it, making her way to a stand of trees. She couldn't say why she had returned, but the sound of the trees in her head had only subsided once she was back outside, shivering in the cold night air.

From behind a ratty pine she studied the side of Jeanette's house, with its peeling paint and dark windows. There were no signs of life. She stepped out of the trees, making her way towards the backyard, but froze mid-step when the back door opened and a figure stepped out, a long metal flashlight in hand. Deirdre stumbled backwards, eyes darting side to side, desperately searching for an escape. Turning away from the glinting light, she held her breath and ran for the trees. The beam of the flashlight played over the ground but didn't land on her, and when she made it past the low pines and into the taller trees, the adrenaline in her system was surging. Her breathing was fast and shallow, and her heart raced, pulse pounding in her neck below her ear.

She huddled down, making herself as small as she could, and the flashlight beam danced across the tree line before moving back to the house. Then the footsteps stopped, and the beam pointed downwards. Deirdre peeked around a tree, as slowly and carefully as she could.

Jeanette was older but still clearly recognizable, wearing a white bathrobe and slippers, her blond hair pulled into a ponytail tight enough to make her eyes slightly squinty. She shone the light at the dead strip of lawn around her feet, moving it slowly from side to side as if tracking something.

Suddenly, she hopped quickly onto one slippered foot and hissed, holding her other foot off the ground and shining the flashlight where it had just been. Quietly, but distinctly, in a voice Deirdre remembered well, she said, "What the fuck—" then breathed in loudly and whimpered with a sound that was vaguely canine. She tried to step backwards and fell, the flashlight's beam arcing across the dark sky as she crumpled. Something was wrapped around her ankle, holding her to the ground, and she tried to shake it loose, making shrill yelps of disgust. Then her left wrist snapped downwards, making an audible thud as it hit the ground, and with her free hand she whipped the flashlight beam towards it.

In the harsh white light, it was unmistakable. Whatever had her wrist was moving, tightening, writhing itself around her. She lurched backwards and dropped the flashlight, uttering a string of staccato syllables: *No no no no no*. The flashlight skittered back and forth, bumped and shaken by the motion of her body, and in the chaotic sideways light, dark tendrils emerged from the ground and wrapped themselves around Jeanette's legs, waist, chest. She spasmed violently, but the tendrils multiplied, holding her down. Slowly, the thrashing body was subdued into a weak shudder, a human form enveloped in thousands of twisting, looping strands.

There was a momentary stillness and a strange too-complete silence, then the sound of tearing, like a piece of fabric being ripped in half. As Deirdre watched, unable to look away, the whiplike tendrils yanked Jeanette's meekly struggling body down, tightening and lashing, pulling her flat against the ground. *Roots*, Deirdre thought, as they drew taut and continued tightening, the moonlight glinting off their brown-black sheen. A larger tendril emerged from the ground and coiled around Jeanette's neck with horrific efficiency, causing her eyes to bulge out in terror as her head was wrenched to the ground. Deirdre could see the whites of Jeanette's eyes, and while it was probably just a trick of the moonlight, it seemed Jeanette could see Deirdre as well, and that her look was pleading, more sad than terrified.

Then the roots squeezed in earnest, and Jeanette's body went limp, giving itself over to their relentless pull. Deirdre, involuntarily, remembered a scene from a film she'd once seen. It took place on a farm, where a woman walked to a chicken coop, picked up a chicken, carried it to a stump, and in one seamless sequence of actions, laid it down sideways, wielded an axe, and brought it swiftly down onto the chicken's neck, where the blade planted into the wood with a flat thump. What Deirdre remembered in particular was not the moment of death, but rather the next shot, when the woman hoisted the headless chicken, now swinging freely, a thin line of blood trailing from its neck. It wasn't the violence so much as the uncanniness of the transition from living thing to simply *thing*, from a body taut with intent and force to dead weight. As the roots yanked and dragged Jeanette's body, now simply a thing, it rocked and shook, one free hand waving limply in meaningless gesticulation.

Slowly, almost imperceptibly, the body changed before her eyes. The roots continued to pull in a juddering motion, easing into a slow and sustained hold, then coiling and tightening until the body collapsed into the ground. What had once been Jeanette was growing flatter, less contoured, deflated. *She's being drained.* Deirdre wanted to look away, but her fear of moving was too great, so she witnessed the roots drain—*drink*—the once-varied form into a steadily flatter and smoother mass, until it was little more than a small hillock, one pale hand still intact aboveground at an impossibly skewed angle.

The roots gave a final surge, taking the hillock and hand fully underground. As they retreated back into the earth, a few stragglers remained, moving with a sickening sluggishness, like the drowsiness that follows a large meal. The flashlight rolled slowly to a stop, and in its static beam a dense patch of short grass appeared, dark and vibrant against the dead lawn that surrounded it.

Deirdre remained still, eyes fixed on the ground where Jeanette had been. Her legs ached from squatting behind the tree, and she stood shakily, feeling a deep warmth emanating from the trees at her back. *Dee. Dee. Dee. Dee.* She turned to face them, eyes scanning the thick wall of branches and trunks silhouetted in the darkness. From inside the house, a baby began to cry.

Deirdre didn't remember getting back to the house, only that she had somehow made it upstairs and into the shower, where she rubbed a bar of soap over her skin until it was raw and red. She closed her eyes and let the steam surround her as she scraped the soap over her hands and wrists, dragging tracks into it with her nails. In her mind, she replayed the whipping and grasping roots, heard the sickly cracking of the body collapsing into itself. She felt the smooth plastic of the wreath in her hands, the thrill of taking it from Jeanette's porch and bringing it back here, to the room across the hall, to the closet, and placing it into the damp dirt on the floor.

When the hot water started to run out, she turned off the shower and dried herself slowly with a towel that smelled of detergent and mildew. She used it to dry the steam off the mirror. It must have been nearing sunrise, and while her exhaustion was apparent, she also noticed a hardness around her eyes that she hadn't seen before. She thought past what had just happened at Jeanette's house to earlier in the evening, to the drive to and from the restaurant through the forest. She thought back to the day before, when she'd first seen Milo, remembering his smell as he stepped in to give her a hug. She thought back further, years before, to the day she'd been standing in just a towel, Jeanette's voice harsh and loud enough to break through the slam of locker doors and the shouting that echoed off the concrete ceiling, *Why don't you just leave town already,* the laughter of her friends in tow as they left Deirdre there, clutching the towel, hands shaking with anger.

She examined herself in the mirror again and let the towel drop to the floor, then leaned in closer, enjoying the new hardness around her eyes. She walked straight to the closet in her mother's room, her half-wet feet leaving damp footprints on the wooden floor and thin throw rug. The slatted doors had swung open, pushed from within by lower branches of the tree now billowing outward. The tree was not just wider but taller, reaching most of the way to the high shelf at the back of the closet, the trunk thicker than she remembered. The smell, too, had somehow intensified, and beneath the strong scent of cedar and sap was a deeper smell, something like the first moment after putting a steak on a hot salted pan.

She leaned in to examine the dirt beneath the tree. The wreath, like the pen, had disappeared. She rose and backed away, still facing the tree, noting that it was roughly her height. *Both of us naked.* Her gaze moved from the tree's base to its roots, which twisted and snaked into the darkness of the closet. She recalled the guttural snapping sound as Jeanette had ceased twitching and become merely weight, the deftness with which the root-tendrils had enveloped her into nothingness, the darker, newly growing spot on the dead lawn, shimmering in the light of the moon. Her mind circled back to the locker room, her unsteady hands taking wrinkled, inside-out clothes from her locker piece by piece, struggling to pull them onto her still-wet body. She considered her hands now, in the half-darkness of her mother's old room, and noted how still and steady they were. In front of her the tree's roots curled into an intricate mesh, not unlike the roots that had wrapped themselves around Jeanette's body with such precision and intent. She considered the massive roots of the towering pines in the forest south of town, big enough to make the concrete of the highway lift and buckle, powerful enough to split stone as they reached into the depths of the earth with blind thirst.

She smiled, pulled back the covers of her mother's bed, and got in naked. Despite the coldness of the house, she felt warm and comfortable, and within a few minutes she was fast asleep.

They compose. They fortify. Their bases plummet downwards, plunge into earth, divide into countless tendrils, coiling, twisting, stretching, clinging. Their roots swarm into a labyrinth of spirals and knots, an infinite sea of hyphae thrusting forward in relentless pursuit. Coursing through stone, concrete, steel, timber. To them, veneer is immaterial. They churn and seethe. They work as one, boundless in the soft soil. They surge beneath, thrust upwards, sensing the life-throbs above. Soon. *The notion forms as one thought, and they taste the nearness on their ruddy tongues.*

Deirdre woke from a dreamless sleep and got up, finally feeling cold in the late-morning chill of the house. She put on a bathrobe and slippers, went downstairs to the kitchen, and gazed out the window at the backyard. The square of grass seemed smaller than it had a couple days prior. The trees pushed in, top-heavy, angling towards the house, and their branches cut jagged shapes through the mist. At the far edge of the grass, a metal chair was on its side, as if toppled by the wind.

She was halfway through unwrapping a day-old muffin when she heard a knock at the door. The four solid raps weren't overly loud, but something about them said it wasn't necessarily a social visit.

She opened the door partway and saw Milo, who hadn't taken off his hat or sunglasses. He smiled, but like the knock, it was more business than friendly. She took the initiative and said, coyly, "You knock like a cop."

"Hi, Dierdre," he said, his voice tight. "Mind if I come in?"

She paused for a half-second too long, but brought out her best sincere smile and gestured at her bathrobe and slippered feet. "Sure, as long as you don't mind the informality." She swung the door open and stepped aside, and he walked past her stiffly. When he reached the center of the living room, he took off his sunglasses and inspected the mantel, his eyes resting on the two unburned candles in their holder.

"You just waking up?" he said, glancing briefly at the ceiling before turning his gaze back to her.

Deirdre sensed she should take as casual a tone as she could, but something within her bucked and resisted, resentful of his distinct shift, and she settled on a line she'd heard in dozens of police procedurals. "Is this official business?"

His expression remained stolid. "I'm on the clock, yeah. We got another call this morning. Jeanette Lund didn't show up for her shift at the market."

Deirdre blinked once, slowly, and said, "Huh. Maybe she finally decided to blow this town."

He looked at her flatly, and the two of them stared at each other in silence for a beat. Milo was the first to look away, again casting his gaze up at the ceiling.

"Anyway," she said, "have a seat. Do you want a muffin? I've got a few here I'll probably just end up throwing out when I leave."

He seemed disarmed by the offer, replying with a quiet assent before sitting on the couch. She went to the kitchen and returned with a muffin centered on a plate but still wrapped, placing it on the coffee table in front of him and sitting in a chair across from the couch.

They sat in silence for a moment as he started to unwrap the muffin, easing one side out of the wrapper and taking a bite. Then he set it back onto the plate and straightened, smoothing his shirt. He smiled faintly, and for a moment there was a hint of their rapport from the previous day. When he spoke again, it was with a new tone that was equal parts gentle weariness and cool professionalism. "I really don't know where to start with this. We were just closing the last cases, and now two more people go missing in two days. They're not officially missing persons until 48 hours have passed, but once those first reports come in, pretty much no one suddenly shows up. And with Jeanette, well, the baby complicates things. A neighbor heard him screaming this morning and called us when no one answered the door. He's fine, a little dehydrated and still under observation, but Jeanette doesn't have any relatives that we know of."

Didn't have, Deirdre thought. She frowned and tried to take a conciliatory tone. "I'm sorry. I don't know what else you can do but ask questions and keep an eye out." *Keep an eye out?* A voice in her head, pointed and distant like her mother's, *That's rich.* "I think it's just something about this town. And you know, some of us who disappear really do just leave. Maybe she'll turn up again on a bus ten years from now."

Milo frowned and regarded her with hardened eyes, opened his mouth as if to speak, then took another bite of muffin instead. He crossed his legs and leaned back on the couch. "How's the house since you got back?"

Perplexed at the sudden shift in subject, Deirdre cleared her throat and let her eyes meander across the room. "Fine, I guess. It's weird being back, but everything is pretty much how I remember it."

"Do you need any help clearing it out? Your mom kept it pretty neat, but junk always collects around a place no matter how vigilant you are."

"No, it's fine," she replied warily. "And anyway, it sounds like you've got your hands full."

They were silent for a few moments as Milo took another bite of muffin. He set the remainder back onto the plate with a certain finality, saying, "I think you know your mom called the police department a good number of times. What you might not know"—he put his hands on his knees and leaned forward, with emphasis—"is that she also brought in her share of calls." He paused to scan Deirdre's face, which she kept neutral. "Neighbors complaining mostly, property line issues, the usual waste-of-time stuff you get in a small town. But there were also a few more serious ones. I don't know if you remember Theo Barclay, but he said she basically threatened him in the produce section of Valley Mart, said he'd 'regret screwing her over.' I guess she hired him to fix some things around the house and felt he got a little too creative with the bill. Anyway, not exactly headline news." Deirdre sat silently as Milo continued. "He called it in on a Friday, and on Monday we got a call from his partner that he didn't come in to work. That was it, he never showed up again, and apparently your mother was one of the last people to speak to him. Before he disappeared, I mean."

"She wasn't exactly loved around here," said Deirdre.

"Sure," said Milo, clearing his throat. "And I'm sorry to speak ill of her so soon after . . ." he trailed off. Then, in a voice that was clearly trying to be casual but came out too loud: "But if you do find anything around the house that might be of interest, please let me know." He looked up towards the bedrooms and shifted to a quieter tone. "Like I said, I'd be glad to help you sort through her old stuff. Might help give you some closure."

Deirdre stiffened but remained silent, letting her mind work. She surveyed Milo and something in her shifted. *He's working me. Like a suspect.* She remembered her outstretched hands as she stood before the tree, fingers steady, pulse calm. "Thanks, Miles. I'll let you know. But for now I think you should probably get back to work, and I should probably put on some clothes."

She thought she could see Milo wince ever so slightly as he got up from the couch and walked to the front door. He opened it partway, put his sunglasses back on, said, "See you around, Deirdre Towhee," and walked out, closing the door behind him.

Outside, the mist was still thick, and Deirdre's skin prickled beneath the bathrobe. She stood next to the toppled lawn chair, staring down at the grass. Thoughts churned in her head, snippets of dialogue and snapshots of images rolling over each other. Milo and his newly cold smile. Jeanette's limp hand in the dirt. Her mother's voice echoing in the empty house. The tree pushing upwards in the murky darkness upstairs. *Why don't you just leave town already.* She stared at the grass, tightened the belt of her bathrobe, and began to smile.

The work went quickly despite the cold. The lawn chair had been pushed aside, and the grass gaped open with a dark, muddy wound. Purposefully, with paced intent, she lifted shovelfuls of dark soil one by one, emptying them onto a steadily growing pile, pausing occasionally to catch her breath. Her bathrobe flapped in the breeze, but her skin flushed with sweat and effort. The hole steadily deepened. She dug through topsoil latticed with a tight web of long, thin roots that seemed to have no beginning or end. As she dug deeper, though, the shovel found its way more easily, pushing smoothly through dark, rich earth until the hole was roughly a meter in diameter. The dirt was strangely light for its dampness, and it gave off an undefinable scent of metallic sharpness and decay.

As she dug deeper, new roots appeared, tough and sinewy, too thick to cut with the shovel. She nudged these aside, and they seemed to acquiesce, curling amenably around the edges of the hole. Deirdre's mind was clear now. The echoes had dwindled and the images fallen away, leaving a sharp picture of the single thing she knew she had to do. She tossed the shovel aside and wriggled out of the muddy bathrobe, leaving it in a damp pile on the lawn. Her naked skin steamed in the cold air, and she strode into the house. Upstairs, she found familiar clothes in her room, remnants of her previous life: Carhartt pants, a faded denim jacket, a pair of old hiking boots shaped perfectly to her feet.

Fully dressed, she returned to her mother's room and stared at the tree. She stepped forward and brushed her hand against the upper branches, feeling them follow the movement of her arm and then snap back into place as she raked her fingers through them. The small cedar-needles possessed a strange tackiness that gripped her skin, like rubbing trained velvet in the wrong direction. She paused—not in hesitation, but to inwardly say a small invocation that had spontaneously come to her while caressing the tree, *Life into life*—before grasping the thick trunk just above its base.

The tree was heavy but surprisingly easy to carry, and as she backed away from the closet, fingers wrapped around the trunk, she marveled at how effortlessly the roots trailed out after it, popping free from the corners and cracks into which they had burrowed, retracting into whorls and coils that bounced around her feet. She shook the tree a few times, letting the excess dirt fall to the floor, then walked it sideways across the room and through the door. At the top of the stairs, she paused for a moment to make sure the roots were all trailing properly, then stepped tentatively onto the top step.

She made her way down the stairs and through the living room, and by the time she reached the far wall, she was confident enough in her ability to carry the tree that she reached out with one hand to open the back door without setting it down. She walked down the two concrete steps to the backyard and made her way across the grass, stopping at the far end of the yard near the back fence, at the edge of the hole.

The mist persisted and the air was cool against her skin as she hoisted the tree high, gathering its roots into the hole. Then, slowly, carefully, she lowered it. As its base approached ground level, she pushed soil over the roots with her boot, and when half the dirt pile was depleted, she let the tree rest in place. She took a step back, and the tree shifted slightly in the ground, its branches swaying in the mist. Then it stiffened, shivered with a nearly imperceptible movement, and she watched as the soil churned, roots twisting through loose clumps of earth. *Now you're home*, she thought, and grabbed the shovel. She filled in the rest of the dirt around the tree, propped the shovel against the fence, and smoothed the freshly packed soil with her hand. It was velvety and warm to the touch, and she smiled again. *It won't take long.* A surety beyond certainty.

Still breathing heavily from the effort, she rose and brushed the dirt off her hands, taking in the image of the freshly planted tree. Its gray-blue needled branches formed a darker shape, like a cutout or void, against the backdrop of vibrant green lawn. A light breeze passed, just strong enough to disrupt the fringe of her hair, and as it passed over the tree, the smaller branches were coaxed into rhythmic loops and bounces. The breeze stopped, and the branches eventually came to rest, though she thought she could see a vague shudder in the moment before they were still, like the shiver of a body after stepping out of water.

Her eyes moved to the base of the tree. Though the air was still, fine grains of soil rolled and bounced beneath the lowest branches. She closed her eyes and listened, no longer troubled by the predominant small-town quiet that surrounded her. She listened beyond the silence, and at the edge of her perception noticed a new sound, at first too faint to pick up, but gradually growing into something audible. A sound like trees moving in wind, though instead of a single gusting rise and fall it seemed to have many sources, starting here, stopping there, always just at the edge of audibility. Yet deeper she could hear the distant contours of her name, repeated endlessly in a rough whisper. *Dee. Dee. Dee. Dee.*

Her eyes still closed, she lowered herself onto the grass to wait, feeling it move softly against the back of her neck, her body lifting and lowering subtly as if she were floating on water and some vast undersea creature was passing beneath her.

They surge. They stream. They feel the momentous shift of reconnection, the renewed vigor of roots enmeshed with roots, a tide of regeneration welling in their veins. They move, swiftly now, their roots racing forward, careening towards a center where the life-throbs pool and pulse. Their thirst is voracious, palpable, and it sends the roots scrambling forward, soldiers of the cause. They consume. They grow. They flex with newfound strength, taste the coppery flavors of sustenance, emergence, fortification. They consume, unstoppably. The life-throbs move and thrash, make angular sounds that shear away as the throbbing diminishes. They feed until nothing remains.

The morning mist had burned away, and now the sun bore down from a cloudless sky. Deirdre opened her eyes and squinted against the bright blue clearing above her, fringed with treetops that seemed yet taller since the day had begun. She imagined the sky as ground, and she floated in a sea of evergreen, held up by the soft slope of roots against her back. The last screams had died out some time ago, and the distant air-raid siren of the volunteer fire department had wound down into silence. Even the cacophony of shuddering cracks and snaps had given way to a deep stillness. The smell of pine and sap lingered in the air.

Slowly, she sat up and shook her head. The tree—*her* tree—had grown markedly, its limbs casting a labyrinth of shadows across the grass. All around her, a thin layer of roots covered the ground, shimmering and throbbing, their tendrils curling satedly against each other.

On her way towards town, she followed the meshwork of roots as it thickened, in both number and volume. Saplings sprang from rifts in driveways, and jagged taproots burst through roadway pavement. Fresh treetops crested the roofs of single-story buildings, casting long shadows across their walls, young branches unfurling into the cloudless sky. Pristine needles emerged from their creases, glinting blue-green in the sunlight. At the shuttered auto shop on Main and Douglas, a group of swelling pines broke through the parking lot pavement, causing it to ripple open with a cascade of damp, brassy earth.

Main Street was unrecognizable beneath a solid sheen of root mass. Root tendrils crawled up walls, through windows, past open doorways, over mailboxes and parking meters. The playground pulsed beneath a pliable mat of roots, slide and swing set misshapen silhouettes deformed by knotted strands and budding needles.

In front of the diner, she paused at an empty car covered in dense layers of roots. Its roof protruded upwards in the center, a thick line running straight from left to right side, where she could just make out fragments of blue-and-red plastic that had been cracked and splintered by the force of the roots. *The siren. It's a squad car.* The driver's-side door gaped open, and on the front seat, lying askew on a dark whorl of vegetation, was an olive-green service hat. For the first time, she noticed it was embroidered with the Falls Valley town seal: a pine tree foregrounded against a distant mountain range. She reached out to run her fingers over the gold stitching, but as she did, the tangled roots shrouding the upholstery began to unwind, wriggling upwards to caress her extended hand. The silence seemed to expand around her, seamless and still, complete in its perfection. And with it came a smell, clear and overpowering, the muskiness of wet earth after rain, tinged with smoky sap. The trees shimmered dark green, a newfound verdancy flushing their foliage.

At the south edge of town, Deirdre made her way into the forest, staring intently at her feet as she walked, concentrating on the soft crunch of the pine needles beneath her boots, careful to step around the patchwork of writhing roots. As she reached the edge of the forest, she stopped to examine the canopy of trees overhead. Their needles flushed from blue-green to near black, cycling through waves of color that pulsed upwards to the topmost branches. A sound began to take shape, a trilling that started gently then swelled to an atonal chorus. She turned back to take one last look at the town, scanning the fuzzy outline of empty buildings. *Why don't you just leave town already.*

From the pocket of her denim jacket, she pulled a small branch, barely more than a twig, with fragile whorls of green cedar needles fanning outward from its spine and a wet paper towel wrapped around its base where it had been cut. She turned the branch over in her hand, running her fingers over it, noting the strange gray smoothness of the wood and the way the needles seemed to cling gently to her fingertips. Then she put it back into her pocket and began walking again, crossing the southern border of Falls Valley and stepping into the cool darkness of the forest.

SEQUOIA POINT

Íde Hennessy

*F*ALLING ROCK AHEAD, the neon yellow sign warned, followed by another with an image of a car next to a crumbling cliff. Meg wasn't sure whether to slow down or speed up past the impending possibility of being crushed by an errant boulder.

The destination would be worth the journey, she reminded herself. She knew it had been the other way around for Jeff, a decade ago. He had wanted to travel to Sequoia Point not just because it was a notoriously dangerous place to surf, but because it was so dangerous to get to.

Meg pulled her sunglasses over her eyes for what felt like the millionth time. Sequoia Point Road should have a warning sign for migraineurs, among all the other warnings, she thought. There was something about the dappled flashes of sunlight through trees that reminded her of nightclub strobe lights—not the peaceful drive through the woods she had expected. The tan oaks and towering redwoods were so thick that it was otherwise dark at three in the afternoon, so her eyes had no chance to adjust to those sprays of sunlight bullets around each corner.

Everything about the drive was deeply nauseating, in a way that seemed to well up in her head and radiate to her stomach instead of the other way around. How had she forgotten the crumbling pavement, post-apocalyptic potholes, and hairpin turns? "I guess I blocked this out for the photo ops," she said aloud, wincing at the empty passenger seat. She still wasn't used to traveling alone.

Meg slowed to twenty-five miles per hour as she passed a rusty Volkswagen Beetle nestled forty feet up in the trees. At least there was no bumper-to-bumper Phoenix traffic. She hadn't seen a single other car besides the abandoned Beetle since turning onto this notorious three-hour stretch of switchbacks. Occasionally she'd catch a propane tank, a silvery glimmer of greenhouse, or a skunky whiff of cannabis to remind her of a human presence somewhere in the woods.

The end of the road was spectacular, though, bursting out over the timber lands to a view of the Pacific Ocean and the tiny vacation village of Sequoia Point. There was the little airstrip carved into the hillside, and the single store in town positioned next to it. Meg pulled into its empty parking lot and stumbled onto the asphalt, finally taking a deep breath of salt air.

Her second breath came with a mouth full of hair, and she realized she'd have to wear it short. The old pixie cut Jeff had loved and she had hated. The wind never settled down there, she'd been warned. And it never felt warmer than sixty-five degrees, even in summer—a welcome change from the hundred-degree or more heat that plagued Phoenix for hundred-day streaks.

For now, Meg tucked her wind-whipped hair behind her ears and jammed a yellow knit cap over her brows.

"Come on Meg, *live* a little." Those were her husband's final words to her, and she whispered them like a mantra, her voice drowned out by waves crashing hypnotically on Sequoia Point's rocky shore.

Meg was almost thirty minutes early to meet the realtor—
not as early as planned, but she hadn't taken the road
conditions into account and neither had her nav app,
which had tried to send her off the route several times onto
faded dirt timber lanes or no lanes at all. She'd been warned
about that too, last time they visited, but she thought
perhaps the place had been properly mapped over the last
decade. It was a coastal town in California, after all, not the
goddamn dark side of the moon.

Meg looked at the little cardboard box on the back
seat that contained Jeff's cremains in a Ziploc bag—she
had been surprised when they'd handed it to her, the
banality of it—but she decided to leave it behind for now.
She didn't want to feel rushed, scattering his ashes. She
locked the car, double-checked it, and set off toward the
cliffside trail on foot.

From the single combination store and laundromat, a
narrow street flanked the airstrip, with a long row of beach
houses along the outer edge of cliffs. An obligatory craft
brewery had attached itself to the back of the little store,

like a corrugated-metal and salvaged wood barnacle covered in string lights. She couldn't remember it being there last time, and she couldn't imagine drinking a pint after that nauseating drive. Wine maybe, to calm her nerves and warm her fingers a bit. It looked like it was closed for the winter anyways.

The sky in the west had a metallic quality to it—sun bursting through white and gray in patches, forcing her to squint at the horizon. As she switched to the little foot path along the cliffside clearing, Meg saw several dogs trotting through rock gardens and sniffing at lamp posts—people must let them run loose here in winter, while the cars and tourists are gone, she thought. But was there anyone home in these houses? So many gigantic walls of glass facing the ocean, with blinds and curtains drawn to block out the multimillion-dollar views.

Where the path met back up with the road was a house which had been peculiarly built so that its upstairs windows were facing its neighbors, and none were facing the water. There was just a big blank wall in front, like it had been picked up from somewhere else and plopped down the wrong way by a tornado. She found herself gaping at it for several moments before realizing she was not alone.

"Rich folks are fuckin' weird, right?" said the scruffy man standing in the path a few yards from her, nodding toward the house. He was holding a large laundry bag. "Do you have a cell phone I could use? Pay phone's not working."

Had he just materialized out of some year in which *any* pay phones were still working? Meg took out her cell and unlocked it for him. If he wanted to run off with it, he'd have to drop his laundry, and the phone was a few models behind anything someone would want to steal.

The man was blonde and unseasonably tanned, maybe in his fifties, and wearing shorts despite the weather. She looked around to try to figure out where he'd come from as he dialed, and she spotted a single van in the RV park on the far side of the airstrip. There was a peace sign painted on the back of it, and on the door the phrase *YES TO TREES, NO TO 5G*. This explained the pay phone thing, she thought.

"No idea," the man was saying into her phone as Meg turned her attention back to him. "Nobody else was here . . . No, it's definitely the place."

A brindled pit bull wearing a pink camo collar sniffed at his flip-flops, and he ignored it. Meg watched the dog wander away to the steps leading down to the beach, until the man handed her phone back.

"Thanks," he said, "They call me Elbow. If you need anything." He gestured toward the van.

She smiled tightly and nodded. Jeff would have been sharing a joint with Elbow by now, asking him about the best surf spots, planning a bonfire get-together.

Meg kept walking past the strangely oriented house to where more narrow lanes branched off the main road and wound up through the hills. Some of them, she knew, led to nothing. She could see a couple houses perched high up on the cliffs, though, that made her wonder if the builders knew some great calamity would befall the whole of civilization before they eroded into the sea. The "fuck it houses," she decided to call them.

Meg knew the history of Sequoia Point. In the 1960s, thousands of undeveloped land plots were sold sight unseen to out-of-state buyers hoping to retire on the California coast. But there was a small problem with most of the plots on the steep, rugged coastline: they were completely unbuildable. Buyers who did come to look at the land before purchasing were flown in, so that they were blissfully unaware of how difficult it was to actually get there by land—or by sea.

Though Sequoia Point Road had since been laid with asphalt, it was still considered one of the most dangerous byways in the state. It would get blocked by mudslides every few winters, cutting the town off from the rest of civilization for weeks at a time. With full knowledge of these things, this was where Meg had bought a home to work remotely from.

After circling back to the general store, Meg had to shield her eyes again, this time against the sun's intense reflection on the store's front door. It wasn't glass, but a wooden door with an elaborate mirror design glued to the surface—a series of hexagons, like the eye of an insect under a microscope. An oddly aggressive choice of decoration, but Humboldt County billed itself as having "more artists per capita than anywhere else in California." The cement trash bin and planters outside were also decorated, in less sparkly mosaic ocean scenes.

Meg passed the time she had left eyeing cans of organic vegetables that cost three times what they did inland, while the elderly clerk ignored her. She was amused to discover the store still played what she and Jeff had dubbed "Wishful Thinking Beach Mix." A steady rotation of reggae, Jimmy Buffett, and the Beach Boys strummed in defiance against the silver sky and stinging wind outside.

A corkboard near the register displayed some faded flyers for beach yoga classes and mobile massage, but mostly missing person posters with smiling young people holding surfboards or salmon. *Backpacker, mushroom hunter, cannabis trimmer*, she read.

"Are you Megan?" asked a woman who had just stepped into the store. She wore a purple kaftan with gold trim, and her long gray hair was pulled into two frizzy braids on her shoulders.

"I go by Meg," she corrected.

"You're younger than I thought you'd be," said the realtor, stepping back outside and gesturing for her to follow. "Aren't you a little young to end up here, a single woman?" she went on. Then without giving Meg a chance to reply, "This is me in the Subaru, you follow."

The house was not far, just a few minutes up one of the lanes to nowhere off the main road. There was no view of the ocean, just seemingly endless trees. It was a manufactured home, a glorified double-wide, which had been converted unsuccessfully into a vacation rental. Like most of the land there, it had been a cash-only sale, and she had bought it with only internet photos to judge it by.

The kitchen could be generously described as "open-concept," being half-separated from the living room only by a hanging beach-scene tapestry and a border on the floor where carpet met linoleum. At least the place was already furnished, she thought, as the realtor gave her a tour through rooms with low ceilings, whitewashed wood panels, beige throw pillows, and driftwood-framed signs that said things like *it's wine o'clock somewhere* and *beach bitch*. Meg couldn't imagine towing a U-Haul full of furniture behind her on that torturous drive, so it would have to do.

"Keys," the realtor said, dropping them into Meg's hand. "And before I forget . . ." She dug into her purse and pulled out a quartz crystal on a red ribbon. After removing the *beach bitch* sign from above the entryway, she hung the quartz there instead. "For feng shui."

"Do you want that?" Meg asked, gesturing at the tacky sign in her hand.

"Not a chance." The realtor put it down on the chipped Formica counter, then looked at Meg the way one might look at an overweight cat begging for second lunch. "A bit of advice I share with all my clients: it will never love you back."

"The house?" Meg asked, taken aback.

"This place," Irina said, gazing through the window at the peaceful view of trees and pine needles blanketing the earth. She handed Meg a business card. "I'm in the neighborhood if you need anything. Don't hesitate."

IRINA (JUST IRINA)
Realtor | Tarot
1 PEPPERWOOD LN
Sequoia Point, CA

After pained deliberation, Meg placed the box of Jeff's cremains on the coffee table next to a decorative bowl of cockles, shriveled starfish, and pimpled urchin shells—the remains of the sea he had always been so drawn to.

Under her new hotel-white linens that night, she dreamt she was pregnant again, but further along than she had ever been. Her belly swelled in front of her like a perfect honeydew melon under her shirt, but when she touched it, the skin pressed inward like a deflating balloon.

She was full of air. Why did she feel so *heavy*?

In the morning, Meg wrestled a cup of coffee out of a lopsided French press and poured it in her travel mug to take to the beach. She gave the box of Jeff's ashes an apologetic look from the doorway. She would know when the time was right to take him with her, she told herself.

Mist still clung to the ground in her tiny patch of yard, but thinned out as she walked downhill past several *LAND FOR SALE* signs half hidden in brambles. There was no flat land to speak of, just sheer drops covered in trees and shrubs. She wondered how hard it would be to carve a cave into the cliffside and live like a Neanderthal.

The closest access to the beach below was a steep path of wooden steps jutting out of the hillside. A sign at the top read: *DANGER / STRONG BACKWASH / SLEEPER WAVES / RIP CURRENTS / NO*

LIFEGUARD / SURF UNSAFE, as if someone had been challenged to fit as many warnings as possible onto one sign.

As Meg carefully wound her way down, she remembered the kid on a tricycle who had yelled to her and Jeff, "Just don't go *that* way," pointing to the steps she now walked. She imagined his parents had meant that warning for him specifically, and he was passing it on to everyone as children do. They laughed about it, but she kept her eyes on Jeff that day while she pretended to look at limpets.

The beach was a long strip of volcanic black sands crusted with inky tidepools. The last time she had been there was in summer, when it was crawling with surfers and underdressed tourists in swimsuits, shivering and goose-pimpled. She could almost hear the shrieks of teen girls wading into the water and realizing it wasn't the warm Atlantic.

Meg crouched at the edge of the tidepools, squinting against the glitter of sunlight on the puddles. Jeff had already leapt across them to the ocean's angry edge, and she stood up to follow.

"Careful!" Jeff said, pointing at squishy grey masses covered in bits of shell at her feet. "Anemones and sea snails."

They were everywhere. A little black snail shell popped under her shoe. Meg realized the way to him was an impossible obstacle course of sea life, and she hung back on the black sands.

A six-foot-tall spray of water between rocky outcrops brought Meg back to the present, and she tightened her hood against the winter wind. She made her way along the beach to look for the much-photographed natural archway in the cliffs, only accessible at low tide. That was when she spotted the painter.

The man was wearing an oversized parka and gazing out at a little island of rock coated in white mounds of seagull poop. In front of him was a wooden easel splattered in various shades of gray, green, and blue. At his side, an old golden retriever napped with its head on its paws.

"Good morning!" Meg called out, and he spun around, visibly relaxing when he caught sight of her. "What are you painting?" she asked, thankful to have an easy topic for small talk. Jeff had always been the one to introduce himself to new neighbors or find a way into closed conversations, something that came so naturally to him.

The man stepped in front of the easel, blocking it, and gestured vaguely at the rock island. He seemed about her age, mid-thirties, with a round face and an overgrown ginger beard.

"Do you live in town," she asked, rubbing her hands together to warm them, "or just visiting?"

"Just staying for the winter," the painter said, pointing up at one of the beach houses with its curtains drawn. "Thought I was the only tourist here this time of year."

"Oh, I'm not a tourist. I just moved here," Meg blurted, feeling stupid afterward. She was basically a tourist too, at this point.

"Ah, I'm just here for the winter," the man repeated, looking out at the island again as if someone had just called to him from it.

Meg bent to pet the sleepy dog and stole a glance up at the painting, which was a realistic rendering of the guano covered rock and the sea. It looked like it could be hanging in her failed vacation rental amid the seashell soap dishes and macrame planters, if not for something formless seeping up from the gray water and onto the rock in glow-in-the-dark-green.

"Not what people picture when they think of California, this place," Meg said nervously, and the painter nodded. She decided to leave him alone with his oddly disconcerting art.

On her way back to the path up the cliff, Meg picked up one of the iridescent mussel shells that littered the sand and tossed it as far as she could into the waves. The mussels here were for looking at, not for eating, Irina had told her. Even in winter now, they were tainted by the algae that causes paralytic shellfish poisoning. Meg was a vegetarian, anyways.

Welcome to Sequoia Point, she thought, where everything is out to kill you. But the same could be said of Phoenix these days, with its random mass shootings, overstressed power grid, strict water rationing, and 110-degree midsummer heat. And she was never going back.

At home that night, Meg poured herself a glass of pinot and sat down with the leather-bound Guest Book the seller had carelessly left in the house. Not an especially thrilling read, it was mostly variations on "thank you for the peaceful getaway" with some gentle suggestions: "more toilet paper," "another space heater." One guest complained about "horrible noises" outside at night and "homeless rummaging in the yard."

Then she came to a guest who had apparently mistaken the book for a personal diary.

Lovely day. Saw bright orange starfish and purple anemones in the tidepools.

Meg skimmed through a couple pages detailing what the writer ate at the brewery for each meal, various types of birds they spotted, and what the weather was like. Then things got weird.

There is something incredibly wrong with this place.

This appeared to be the same writer, and the same distinctive turquoise pen, but the cursive had gotten looser. Everything after was illegible, the sort of shorthand only the writer of it can understand. The cursive on the next couple pages was just a leading letter and a flat or vaguely wobbly line. The only word she could make out at all was what looked like *noon* or *moon*.

A low thumping sound outside made Meg spill the wine on her shirt, and she got up to investigate, cursing her nerves. On second thought, she grabbed a dull chef's knife from the kitchen, feeling silly about it but not silly enough to go without.

Meg swung open the front door and at first she saw nothing, until the sound started up again. She looked down to see it was the painter's dog, its wagging tail thumping against the wall outside.

"Where the hell did *you* come from?" she asked the smiling old dog. "Let's get you home."

Meg was happy to have an excuse to leave the house, despite the setting sun and the deeper chill that came with it. She convinced the dog to hop ungracefully into her backseat, then drove downhill toward the beach house its person had pointed out earlier.

"Hello?" Meg called out after knocking several times on the nautical-blue painted door. She could hear that someone was home, so she waited.

The painter opened the door a crack, wedging his body in the doorway as if to keep her from seeing inside. Probably binge drinking, she thought, picturing empty bottles everywhere. A tragic artist. A lost weekend.

"Yes?" The painter's face was ruddy and tired.

"Your dog." She gestured to her stinky companion. "He showed up at my door."

"Ah, sorry about that." He reached his hand toward the old beast, who let out a low growl and slunk backwards. "He gets—"

A loud crash from somewhere in the house made him whirl around, and Meg asked, "Everything alright in there?"

"Yes, yes, it's just the dog," he said. "I'd better go see what he's up to."

Meg stood there for several moments after he closed the door, unsure what to do. Did he have more than one dog? She looked at the one that was still cowering behind her.

"You stay here." She tried to sound commanding. "Stay!"

Meg was sure the painter would realize soon enough that he had left his pet on the wrong side of the door. She knocked lightly again before slipping away, hoping not to make things too awkward.

As she drove back up the hill, Meg's phone lit up.

Her mother.

Meg let it go to voicemail and played it back.

"Meggie, give me a call back this time, please. I'm worried about you . . . I don't understand this whole move to California thing. There's earthquakes and break-ins and . . . tent cities everywhere, for God's sake."

Meg hit delete.

Sunday morning called for another walk to the beach. Maybe she would go further this time, to the other side of the archway, if the tide was low enough. As she climbed down the steps, she heard the unmistakable barking of sea lions. A small colony had taken up residence on the rocky island the artist had been painting the day before.

She flinched as a large wave broke onto the rock, exploding salt spray twenty feet into the air, but the sea lions barely seemed to notice. Some flopped onto their other side, and some couldn't be bothered to stir at all.

As Meg walked below the empty beach houses, she spotted several skeletons of creatures not immediately recognizable, as if they'd been re-arranged artistically in the sand. Was that a bird's head paired with a fish body? Who had gone to all this trouble?

She soon had her answer when she crossed the soggy littoral zone to where the famous archway was now visible. The red-haired artist was standing on a large volcanic rock in front of it—completely nude. His pale, freckled skin almost glowed in the wintry sunlight, and she wondered how he wasn't shivering at all. Perhaps he was partaking in something stronger than alcohol.

He turned to look in her direction, without seeming to see her.

"Oh!" She instinctively put a hand up to cover her eyes and turned her head. "I'm sorry, I wasn't expecting . . ."

No reply. When she stole a glance back at the archway, there was no one there. Just a gull pecking at something on the rock where the man had been standing. But he had to be somewhere close—*hiding?* Meg tried to appear unshaken as she hurried away, toward the hopefully less strange company she would find at the market.

"Morning," Meg said to the elderly clerk, picking up a bottle of locally made kombucha and trying to sound chipper. "Where would I find avocados?"

The clerk gestured toward the back of the store. "Ask *him* if he'll share—he just picked up the last ones."

She glanced back to see the artist in his oversized parka and paint splattered jeans, a basket of groceries hanging off his arm.

The kombucha slipped from Meg's hand and hit the floor with a crack and fizz. Its gelatinous scoby slid across the tiles like some gruesome sea slug from a broken aquarium.

"I'm sorry," Meg stammered, bending to pick up the pieces of glass, but the clerk grabbed a mop from behind the counter and gestured her away.

There was *no way* the artist had dressed himself so quickly and beaten her here—unless he could teleport. "I'm sorry," she repeated, to him this time, "but do you have a twin brother?"

The artist set his basket down on the counter and watched the clerk impatiently. "No, of course not."

Outside the market, with a bag full of groceries sans avocado, Meg ran into Elbow again.

The older man was sitting on the edge of a mosaic planter, putting a swirly glass pipe and lighter back in his pocket. "Hey, how's things, uh—"

"Meg," she offered quickly, "and other than feeling like I'm losing my mind, things are going well I guess."

Elbow nodded. "You know what's good for that? Wading out in the water here. The cold'll knock the crazy right out of you."

"Can I ask you something?" Meg knew it was ridiculous, but she couldn't help herself. "Does 5G make people . . . see things that aren't there?"

Elbow leaned toward her and lowered his voice. "No, man. 5G *keeps you from seeing things* that *are* there." Then he sat up straight again and assured her, "There's no 5G here, though. One of the few places left without it."

As Meg was prepping a salad later that afternoon, the realtor paid her a visit, colorful ceramic plate of brownies in hand.

"Are those, umm, medicated?" Meg asked, waving her inside. "I don't think I should—"

Irina laughed, patting her on the arm. "No, I keep those ones for myself."

"Do you want to join me? I don't have much of an appetite—"

"I just came by to check on you," Irina said, looking around the room. "See how you're settling in."

Meg's lip trembled and she bit it, turning away to swirl some inky vinegar into a platter of olive oil.

"That good, eh?" Irina set her straw tote bag on the counter and pulled something wrapped in newspapers out of it. "Maybe you could use this."

Meg unwrapped the papers to reveal a stoneware jar with a perfectly rounded face carved into it; it was topped with a cork. "It's beautiful . . . Is it decorative, or what should I use it for?"

Irina was casually rearranging some kitschy trinkets on the windowsill into a more symmetrical order. "Have you heard of a witch bottle?" she asked. Meg shook her head, and the older woman went on. "It's a talisman for luck. For protection."

Meg supposed the feng shui crystal wasn't enough in her case. "I see. Thank you, Irina."

"There are instructions inside. You have to do it *before* the full moon, though. It's very important."

Meg humored her. "Alright, when is that?"

"Two days from now." Irina picked up her purse and headed toward the door, turning back once to say, "Don't forget."

Alone with her salad, Meg drank a little too much cabernet franc that night. When she woke to the sound of someone trying her doorknob, she was groggy and unsteady on her feet.

Squatters? Someone who thought the house was still a vacation rental, looking for an easy burglary? Her car was parked outside though, so clearly the house wasn't vacant. Irina was the only one who knew where she lived—maybe she had accidentally left something here earlier . . . but why wouldn't she knock? Why try the doorknob?

She thought of the artist earlier, pale and naked, something *wrong with his eyes.*

"Jeff!" Meg yelled, pretending to alert her husband. Whoever it was outside didn't need to know she was alone with a box of ashes. "Will you get the rifle and go check the door?"

There was no rifle. Thank goodness all her blinds were closed. With the ocean view hidden by trees up here, she had taken a cue from the other residents and closed her home off to the prying eyes of seagulls and whatever else might be out there in the off-season.

She tried to make herself sound heavier as she made her way to the front door. Through the peephole, she could see the pebble path lit ghostly-blue by fading solar lanterns. Nobody was there.

A gust of wind rattled the windows and she jumped back, steadying herself on the kitchen island. Maybe that was what she had heard earlier—only the wind—as much as it had sounded like a person rattling the doorknob. She wasn't used to the sounds of this cheaply manufactured home yet.

In the morning, hungover, Meg called out of work, claiming her body wasn't used to the California germs yet. She never called out of work at home.

Home? *This* was home now, she reminded herself.

After a long shower and a cup of coffee with oat milk, she uncorked Irina's housewarming gift. There was a thin red candle and a rolled piece of paper inside the stoneware jug, so she patted it on the bottom like a bottle of ketchup until they fell out.

IRINA'S CREATIONS

irinascreations4u.net

Use this bottle to collect the urine of the person requiring protection.
Add a lock of their hair, three nails, and a pinch of salt.
Re-seal the bottle with wax (enclosed).
Bury the bottle on your property, on a day with a waxing (NOT WANING!) moon.
Moon Phase calendars are available for purchase at the link above.

How much urine, Meg wondered. The amount you need for a urine sample at a doctor's office? A memory thawed inside her, of a suffocating white room. A nurse talking about her "new adventure," about pre-natal needs. Meg banished the image with a deep breath, then sipped more coffee while looking through drawers for any stray nails.

Nothing. There were a couple plastic thumbtacks still stuck in a seashell-framed corkboard next to the bathroom, though. She found a third one holding up the *it's wine o'clock somewhere* sign and tossed the sign on the counter with its *beach bitch* sibling.

The urine part was messy. The bottle opening was a much smaller diameter than a collection cup, and she hoped she had gotten enough into the damn thing after getting so much of it on her hand.

She set the bottle on the bathroom floor, repulsed by the thought of a jug of urine on her counter, and scrubbed her hands with soap twice.

Looking at her long, tangled hair in the mirror, Meg thought about the relentless winds outside. She wasn't ready for another pixie cut, but now seemed like as good a time as any to give herself bangs. She combed her hair out and pulled some of it forward over her face like a horror movie hag. She twisted a handful in front the way she had seen in hairstyle tutorials, and snipped.

"Oh, God."

Not exactly the carefree, choppy fringe Meg had seen in influencers' videos. She looked like she had cut her bangs with a little salad bowl.

She stuffed the hair clippings into the jug of urine, added the thumbtacks, and then a pinch of salt. She hoped

Himalayan pink salt would work—the general store had been out of regular.

Work to do *what?* She wasn't sure, exactly. A calming placebo effect? But it surely couldn't hurt.

The ground of her tiny allotment was gravelly and heavy with clay this high up in the hills, but luckily the seller had left a hand spade in the potting shed. She knelt in the pebbles and pine needles, stabbing at the dirt until she had a hole roughly bottle-sized.

Something crunched closer to the house, startling her, and she dropped the spade.

It was just a deer, a young buck, staring at her from the front path as if she was doing something completely deranged.

This wasn't Meg's first deer encounter, but she felt very small and defenseless kneeling alone in the dirt. She stood up and waved her arms around, trying to make herself appear larger, as if the deer was a bobcat in the Arizona desert.

The buck shook his head in a blur of antlers and turned to hop away, black tail raised to show the snow-white fur beneath it.

"Don't be judging me," Meg called after him. "You don't know what I've been through."

She knelt again to bury the stoneware jug, still nauseatingly warm in her hands.

Meg took another walk down the bramble-lined road to what passed for town. Living in a new place, she hoped to develop new habits. To be the sort of person who went for a walk every day. To work her way up to jogging, even— something she hadn't been able to do in the Phoenix heat.

She could see her breath in the morning here, a reminder that she was alive and warm inside, as cold and numb as she felt on the outside.

Her knees protested the steep downhill climb, though, still used to flat suburban sidewalks. She rested at a picnic table in front of the quaint old lighthouse at the edge of the cliffs, watching sea lions chase gulls from their rocky turf on the beach below.

The sound of someone shouting in the distance drew her attention to the direction of the brewery, where Irina and the artist were engaged in heated conversation outside. She couldn't tell what they were saying, but it seemed dramatic and private enough that she felt compelled to duck behind the picnic table.

At one point, the artist pushed Irina away from him and Meg wondered if she should intervene, but the artist turned away and stomped off toward the general store. Irina spat in his direction, collected herself, and drove off in her Subaru which had been parked in the lot.

A lovers' quarrel? Irina was maybe thirty years older than the man, but still attractive in that "is it yoga or is it plastic surgery" way.

Or maybe a real estate deal gone wrong? There was certainly a lot of potential for that here.

It was none of Meg's business, whatever it was. She had known little of her neighbors in Phoenix, except for makes and models of cars, who kept their lawns mowed, who had ripped them out and put in native plants in defiance of the HOA, who had replaced them with black plastic weed-cloth and red lava rocks. Jeff had been the one with all the inside knowledge on neighborhood drama.

The moon was too bright that night. Meg drew her blinds against the almost perfect orb in the distance, but she could still see it burned into the backs of her eyelids when she closed her eyes.

Again, she heard something in the front yard, but she pulled the blanket over her head this time.

She pictured the black-tailed buck turning away from her, over and over again, to hop into the woods.

"Go away," she said, but no sound came out.

Meg called out of work again the next day. She didn't really need to work anymore, but it was a connection to the world outside the Lost Coast. The un-lost world of corporate offices and chain restaurants and charity "fun-raisers" and keeping up appearances.

The house was beginning to feel small, with its too-low ceilings, and when her gaze fell on the box of Jeff's cremains, it felt even smaller somehow. Despite it being winter, Meg couldn't help but feel nervous about the lack of air conditioning and ceiling fans, something she couldn't imagine living without in Phoenix. She put on a coat and took her coffee outside to sit on the front steps.

Two sips in, she saw it: the stoneware "witch bottle" nestled in a bed of pine needles, next to a mound of dirt.

The artist's golden retriever must have returned for a visit and dug it up—or maybe one of the other loose dogs she had seen wandering around near the shop. Why were there so many loose dogs in this place, anyways? Who did they belong to?

Meg knelt on the dewy earth and buried the bottle again, tamping down the soil with her bare hands. She looked for the largest rock she could find lining her front path, then hammered it down over the hole she had dug, like a gravestone.

The following morning, on her walk, Meg was surprised by a plane overhead, sounding like it might brush the tops of the trees. She picked up the pace, jogging as fast as she could to try to catch its landing at the airstrip. She watched the little Cessna from a safe distance in the field lining the main road, as it touched down and cruised smoothly to a stop.

Jeff had been working on his pilot's license, or Sport Pilot Certificate, as he kept correcting her. She had never flown with him—he wasn't allowed to have passengers yet, which she had been secretly grateful for—but she once watched from the lounge in the tiny municipal airport of Glendale, Arizona. Its claim to fame was "the finest flying weather in the world," with 350 days of clear skies on average each year. *Three hundred and fifty days without rain.* It sounded different now, in the context of dangerously dwindling groundwater reserves.

Meg busied herself while he flew by looking up statistics on plane crashes versus motorcycle accidents, reminding herself that every moment in the air was a moment her husband wasn't on his goddamn bike.

Jeff's ultralight plane bounced off the asphalt—once, twice, three times—like gravity had rejected it. Like the clear blue sky had claimed him as one of its kind, and didn't want to give him up.

But aside from that hiccup or three, it had all gone fine. He climbed out of the cockpit and punched the air, laughing. He picked her up in the airport lounge and kissed her as if he'd just returned from a war of his own making. She could still feel the beard he was growing at the time, wiry against her chin.

The people who emerged from the Cessna in Sequoia Point were less excited. They fought with suitcases and argued with each other. A man and a woman, maybe a decade older than her, both in expensive-looking athleisure, followed by a teenage girl in a ripped black sweater and leggings. The girl's bright blue hair was perfectly bobbed, with rounded bangs like a retro wig.

It *was* a wig, Meg saw, as the wind plucked it off the girl's head and sent it tumbling down the runway like an excited little dog that escaped its leash.

"I *hate* this fucking *place*," the now bald teen shouted as she chased it.

The adults caught Meg watching them and waved. The man gave an embarrassed shrug.

"Do you need any help?" Meg offered. That's what Jeff would do. He would insist on carrying at least two pieces of luggage. The heaviest ones.

"No, I made sure we packed light for once," the dark-haired man said as they walked over to her. He held out a hand. "I'm Ronaldo. This is my wife Louise, and that's our daughter Emma over there."

"I'm Meg. I just moved in up the hill."

"Oh, *permanently*?" Louise asked, her face Botox-bland but her voice betraying surprise.

"We have a summer home here," Ronaldo said, before Meg could answer. "I know what you're thinking—it's winter. But Emma needed a place to recover without all the . . . drama."

"A place to grow her hair back," Louise said, pointing at her own blonde ponytail. Then she whispered, "Chemo," as if saying it too loud might attract the fury of some ancient god of cancer. Meg pictured the three of them turned into pillars of tumors instead of salt. Columns of flesh on the runway, bubbling and replicating and reaching for the sky.

"Hey," Emma said as she joined them, rolling suitcase in tow. She had given up on wearing the wig, thrusting it under one armpit.

"Nice to meet you, I'm Meg." She wanted to tell the girl how beautiful she looked. How stupid she herself had looked in comparison, when she'd drunkenly let Jeff shave her head. How her scalp had been weird and wavy, her forehead too high. But she didn't.

The family—the Garcias—owned one of the beach houses along the cliff, next door to the house the artist was renting. They told Meg to come by any time, the way people do without really meaning it.

"Do you have any bourbon?" Meg asked the elderly employee of the general store. "Buffalo Trace?" She hadn't been able to find any on the shelves. She wasn't much of a whisky drinker, but that had been Jeff's go-to.

"Only got Jim Beam," the white-haired man said, his eyes judging her under their weedy, overgrown brows. He looked suspiciously at the cardboard box she had tucked under her shoulder, then pulled a bottle from the shelves behind him. "This okay?"

"Sure." Meg paid him and took the bottle in its plain paper bag. "I'll get some peanuts too." Despite there being no one around to cast judgement, she didn't want to walk out with just a bottle of liquor concealed in a scrunched-up brown paper sleeve, like a man whose wife has just been killed by the bad guys in an old B-movie. One who's been kicked out of every bar already, to a soundtrack of sad synthesizers and screeching saxophones. A momentary lapse of sense, until he stumbles past a karate dojo and turns to look back at the sign, eyes sparkling with newfound purpose.

Meg had planned to watch the sun set from the beach tonight, then finally scatter Jeff's ashes under the full moon. But when she got to the staircase, she saw how high the tide was.

"The *moon*," she said aloud to no one. She had forgotten its effects on the sea. The water had swallowed most of the black sands in white froth, leaving a dry strip around the steps. She hated to admit it, but she was grateful for the delay in her plans. She sat on a step halfway down, set the box of Jeff beside her, and poured some bourbon out in the ice plants crawling down the cliff.

"I know," she said. "Sorry it's not your brand, love." Then she took a sip for herself.

The moon had been full when Jeff proposed to her on the beach below. But it had been just a soft glow through low clouds. And the beach had been so much larger, ten years ago, before all the sea level rise. They brought flashlights and a cooler down the steps for a midnight picnic. Jeff lit a fire, and that's when they realized they were not alone.

There was an entire herd of deer on the beach, and some of them were in the water, as if it was the most normal thing in the world for them to swim in the ocean.

The head of a large buck burst through the waves, seaweed tangled in its horns like a crown. Meg's breath caught in her chest, afraid he would be pulled back under, but the buck calmly swam back to the beach with the rest.

She and Jeff had watched in silent awe, squeezing each other's hands until her fingers ached, while the herd moved further up the sand and out of sight.

The proposal hadn't been planned. Jeff didn't have a ring, so he tried to tie a piece of dune grass around her wrist instead. It resisted his best efforts, flopping and finally breaking in half while they both laughed about it. They tangled themselves together in a drunken knot on the beach instead, and Meg still cringed when she thought of the sand lodged into every fold of her flesh. Jeff hadn't been bothered at all, like his whole body was a callous.

A sound from the beach below made Meg freeze with the Jim Beam bottle to her lips—it was the anguished yelp and scream of a dog in pain. The sound of something under attack and desperate to get away. Not a dog, she realized—a sea lion.

She twisted the bottle cap on, picked up Jeff, and hurried up the steps, away from whatever would assault something so large and dangerous. Most likely another sea lion—or one of the wandering dogs? She pictured the brindled pit bull from the other day, its dark mouth frothing like the sea foam on the black sands. Rabid, running to jump at her throat.

Meg was asleep in bed, turned away from the window and its drawn blinds, when she was awakened by the sharp thwack of something slamming into the glass.

An owl? She sat up, heart racing, waiting for her eyes to adjust from the world of dreams to the real one. The light switch seemed so far away while she was half asleep.

But then it occurred to her: she didn't want to be seen. What if it *wasn't* an animal? What if someone *had* been trying her doorknob the other night?

Meg tugged her robe off the chair next to her bed and put it on. She crouched on the carpet and crawled to the window, then pulled up the lower-left corner of the blinds, enough to peek outside.

There was no stunned owl or other bird on the ground below the window. And she could see nothing but hazy stripes of tree trunks through fog in the distance.

What if it had been a mountain lion? A bear? They were rare here, allegedly. More likely to be a deer or raccoon.

Meg wasn't going to get back to sleep, so she decided to check all the windows instead. She left the lights off and tiptoed to the bathroom across the hall to peer through its tiny, sideways slider.

Nothing but trees and a glimpse of the lonely roadway.

In the kitchen, the electric oven's clock blazed neon red through the dark: *03:33*. The numbers floated in front of her eyes when she looked away, and she wanted to believe there was some hidden message in them from Beyond, but she knew there wasn't.

She opened the blinds and looked out the kitchen window. Skeletons of blackberry brambles. Trees and mist. She burped involuntarily, her breath releasing a bourbon-scented ghost of hours past.

"Fuck it." Meg flipped the kitchen light switch on, blinking against its fluorescence. She turned on all three faux-coral table lamps in the living room, almost knocking one of them over in the process.

Sleep should come easier to her here, with neighbors too far away to wake her with their screaming fights and late-night lawn mowing "to beat the heat." But every little noise had her jumping to attention.

You'll settle in, she told herself. It was just new-house jitters—not knowing what was normal here yet.

In reply to this, a crash sounded from the direction of the potting shed, as if one of the long-dead, unidentifiable plants had jumped off its stand in protest of her presence.

Meg ran to the front door to look through the peephole, which didn't give her a view of the shed—but close enough, she hoped. She expected to catch a glimpse of the young buck from yesterday morning, doing what any teen boy would do in the middle of the night: making mischief.

There was nothing moving out there, from what she could see through the fog, so she grabbed an empty pan from the stove and a metal soup ladle to bang it with.

Outside, the cold stung her face and prickled the bare strips of skin between her robe and slippers. But she left the door ajar. She didn't want to be fumbling with a knob like people did in horror films, if she was chased by a mountain lion or bear. As unlikely as that was.

She stayed on the lit front path for as far as she could, then carefully made her way to where she could see the shed. Everything was quiet and still now.

Meg banged on the pan for a while, just in case, but no animal dashed away into the woods. Satisfied, she headed back toward the house and nearly tripped over something.

It was the rock—unmistakably the same one she had placed over the fresh dirt that morning. Someone had moved it.

Not just the rock. A broken piece of the stoneware jug, its moonlike, carved face staring up at her.

Meg backed away from the shed and made her way slowly up the path. Never run from predators, she knew that. Don't turn on that switch in their brain that says *dinner*. If whatever had dug up the bottle was still around, she didn't want it to know she was nothing more than a giant rabbit with opposable thumbs and a higher vocabulary.

She slammed the front door behind her, locked the deadbolt, and turned around to see someone staring at her.

Her own goddamn reflection in the kitchen window. She wanted to throw the soup ladle at it but forced a laugh instead, as if her reflection might be disappointed. She put her makeshift drumstick back on the counter, next to the Jim Beam.

"Nightcap?" she asked, watching herself raise the bottle.

Feeling sufficiently heavy with booze, Meg returned to her bedroom and looked through the nightstand, hoping to find something to read herself to sleep. What she found instead was a silk sleep mask in the top drawer. It was stuffed with herbs—something sweet, something pungent, and a stale herbaceous scent she couldn't place. A little paper tag in the drawer informed her:

Complimentary for Guests
from IRINA'S CREATIONS
Cannabis, Chamomile & Mugwort Sleep Mask
~ locally grown ~

Meg put the mask over her eyes and relaxed, picturing herself falling into the too-soft mattress topper, through a tunnel of downy white feathers to a perfect black void at the end.

This time, she woke to the gentle bounce of some weight being lifted from the foot of the bed. "Jeff? Where are you going—"

Jeff wasn't here.

Meg swiftly pulled her knees up under the covers, away from the foot of the bed, and sat up. She couldn't see anything at all, until she remembered the mask and removed it.

There was a *woman* in the doorway. Silhouetted in the dull blue light from the bathroom window across the hall. Petite, like Meg.

"Irina?" Meg grabbed her phone from the nightstand and shook it to turn the flashlight on. It swept across pale, bare breasts topped with an inverted triangle of freckles. Meg steadied the phone and pressed herself against the headboard. "*Who* the *fuck?*"

The woman was completely nude and smudged with wet soil. She was Meg's height. She had Meg's slender arms and disproportionately ample hips. She had Meg's hair, down to the poorly cut bangs, with leaves tangled in it.

She had Meg's *face*. The only difference was her eyes, like someone had added a thin wash of white paint over them.

Meg grabbed her empty water glass and tried to smash it on the nightstand, but this was more difficult than she expected it to be. She held the intact glass in front of her like she was daring the woman to come any closer.

Or *what?* Meg thought.

The woman cocked her head to the side to examine the glass, like a dog trying to decide if something is a danger, a toy, or a treat.

Meg raised the makeshift weapon. The woman winced, putting a hand up in front of her face. And that was all Meg could take. She let the glass fall from her hand onto the bed, the hard knot of fear inside her softening into a yarn ball of concern in her belly. She wouldn't—couldn't—hurt this woman.

The other Meg's skin was a galaxy of spider veins and goosebumps, her lips the color of a fresh bruise. She was holding a beige throw pillow with the word *LIVE* embroidered on it—part of the obligatory *LAUGH* and *LOVE* set. She hugged it to her chest, shivering.

"You're cold," Meg said, her voice still hoarse with sleep. She followed the woman's gaze to the empty glass. "You're thirsty?"

The other Meg was silent, watching her like a curious crow, while Meg pulled the comforter off the bed and draped it over her shoulders. Other Meg dropped the pillow unceremoniously on the floor and pulled the comforter tight around herself.

Meg squeezed past her in the doorway and beckoned her down the hall to the kitchen, while the woman followed in a strange, stuttering tiptoe behind. Like she wasn't used to having legs—or using them to stand and walk.

Like a baby.

"Here." Meg tried to hand her a glass of water from the tap, but the woman's hand stayed balled into a fist around the comforter, and the glass plunked against it. Meg demonstrated drinking a sip before trying again.

She took it cautiously this time and sniffed it, then threw her head back and downed the whole thing in hiccupping gulps.

"I'll take that when you're—"

It was too late. The woman dropped the glass on the tile when she was done, and it shattered next to her bare foot.

"Fuck. *Don't move*." Meg found a broom and a dustpan in the hallway closet, and when she returned the other woman was no longer there.

For a moment, Meg thought—hoped—she had been walking in her sleep, perhaps a side effect of the herbal sleep mask, and she had imagined her double. Until she heard a creak from the living room. The other Meg was crouching on the sofa, back hunched under the down comforter like an enormous white owl.

Meg swept up the wet shards of glass and went back to check on her. "Who are you?" she asked, trying to sound as gentle as possible. *What* are you, is what echoed in her head.

The other Meg picked up a dried starfish from the bowl of shells on the coffee table, tore a piece off it with her teeth, then crinkled her nose and coughed it up on the carpet.

"You don't understand a word I say, do you?" Meg couldn't fathom why, but she felt an overwhelming sense of responsibility for the mysterious woman. Isn't that what happened when a person rescued someone? Stop someone from jumping off a bridge, and it's suddenly your responsibility to make sure they never do it again? But she hadn't rescued this woman. Had she?

What are you?

"I take it you're hungry?" Meg retrieved the bag of peanuts from the kitchen and poured them into a bowl— a plastic one this time, in case the woman decided to chuck it at the floor too. She held it out to the other Meg, who ignored it in favor of tasting the leather-bound guest book.

Meg put a few roasted peanuts in her mouth and chewed them enthusiastically while her double watched with the suspicion of a cat being offered anything but its favorite treat. She put the bowl down on the table and backed away to give her space.

The other Meg grabbed a fistful with grubby fingers, chewed them for a couple seconds, and spat them back into the bowl.

Meg went through everything in the fridge and cupboards, which wasn't much—leftover salad, low-fat granola breakfast cereal, oat milk, saltine crackers, a can of tomato basil bisque. The other Meg wouldn't keep any of them down.

"Well, that's it." Meg put a lid on the pot of soup and stuffed it in the fridge. "Store doesn't open till morning."

Her double watched from a squat on the floor while Meg tucked a fresh sheet into the sofa cushions and draped a blanket over it. She pointed at the other woman, then patted the sofa, hoping to convince her to settle down and sleep.

Meg turned off the lights and headed back to her own room, her eyelids and limbs suddenly heavy, like she was fighting her way through a sedative-belching bog and losing.

Meg woke in a sweat and wondered if she'd left the space heater on, but it sat black and lifeless in the corner. She looked at her phone: *10:14 am*. Her room was unseasonably warm, and her bangs had plastered themselves to her forehead in the night.

Jeff.

She had left him on the coffee table with that *thing* with her face, Meg realized in a panic, as a tide of memories from the night before crashed in waves against her throbbing brain.

She put on her robe and stumbled as quickly as she could to the living room, to find herself alone. Jeff's box was untouched on the table, and the blanket from the sofa was bunched up on the floor, along with the comforter the woman had been wearing.

Everything else seemed to be as she'd left it, including the dirty dishes in the sink from all the food her visitor had refused.

Meg showered off the bourbon scented sweat and pulled out her unopened box of summer clothes. It had to be almost seventy degrees out—why was it *so warm* on this winter morning?

She had her answer when she stepped outside. The usual glowing white clouds above were the color of ashes now. The air was uncharacteristically still, the woods quiet. She pulled up her weather app and a red banner flashed at her.

THUNDERSTORM WATCH

Atmospheric conditions are favorable for the development of severe thunderstorms in your area.

Be prepared and stay alert for changing conditions.

Meg pictured her visitor from the night before, naked and shivering, caught in a torrent of rain. Clutching the *LIVE* pillow like a teddy bear, soggy against her chest. And again, that illogical surge of responsibility washed over Meg. She had to find her. And then she would worry about what to do with her. Who to phone.

She walked around the house, thought of calling out to the woman—but what name would she shout into the woods? Surely not her *own*.

When Meg reached the potting shed and looked behind it, what confronted her was an impossibility—a malign incursion into the relative safety of daylight from the darkest thickets of night.

Meg's own face looked up at her, smeared from chin to nose in a thick stroke of red. Her chest was no longer bare, but dark and sticky with blood, which had glued pine needles to her skin like bristly hairs.

She was kneeling over the young black-tailed buck, his three-point antlers unmistakable.

Meg couldn't focus her eyes on anything for more than a second. Glistening entrails like a pile of eels nipping at the woman's knees. Deep gouges like something had ripped the deer's flesh off with sharp teeth—on his legs, neck, back. No, not teeth. Like acid had gnawed through the bone to marrow. Lifeless brown eyes, wide in a permanent recording of terror on a convex screen.

Don't run.

Don't run.

Meg couldn't move her legs at all, much less run. Luckily, it was the other Meg who jumped to her feet and bounded into the woods, as if something had called to her in a frequency Meg couldn't hear. She was faster than Meg. Stronger too, if she was the one who had taken down the deer.

No, she must have found it that way. She *must* have.

When Meg regained control of her muscles enough to retreat from the gruesome scene, she found something she hadn't noticed earlier: a crocheted hacky sack ball with a green cannabis leaf design on it, sitting next to the *GOOD VIBES ONLY* doormat. It was dark and wet with blood.

With her deadbolts and all of her windows locked, Meg pulled out her laptop. There was only one internet provider here, and it was slower than she had expected it to be, considering how expensive it was.

117

Sequoia Point missing persons, she typed into the search bar.

Do you mean Alderpoint missing persons?

The search result suggested a series of articles on "Murder Mountain" in Alderpoint, about an hour and a half inland. Mostly crimes related to black-market cannabis grows.

"Sequoia Point" missing persons, Meg tried, then clicked the top result, which pulled up a blog called *PERIL NORMAL.* A stock photo of the rocky archway at sunset filled the top half of the screen, then:

SEQUOIA POINT, CALIFORNIA: A Portal Seeker's Paradise?

Black sands, tidepools teeming with life, craft beer brewed with seawater, and some of the tallest trees in the world—this is what Sequoia Point on the Lost Coast is known for. IF you can stomach the infamous winding drive to get there. But what makes this place interesting for our purposes is the significant magnetic anomalies on the map below. Pair that with a lack of 5G radiation, and you've got a possible paradise for paranormal research.

As expected, there's a high number of missing person cases in relation to the tiny population there. I'll be getting a crew together this month to see what we can find. Stay tuned, paranormies!

The words *missing person cases* were a hyperlink, so Meg clicked it, hoping it would take her somewhere that made sense. It was another blog, this one called *MURDER HOUND*.

COPYCAT SERIAL KILLERS IN SEQUOIA POINT?

There was a list of names and dates in reverse chronological order, from the current year to 1966. Most of them were labeled "still missing" but some were labeled "found eaten, mysterious circumstances." The "missing since" dates, Meg noted, were mostly in winter months. She clicked the name at the top.

James W. Cardoso
27, Experienced Backpacker & Tour Guide
Still Missing

There was a collage of photos: a muscular man with a trim beard and kind eyes. She recognized one of the images from the corkboard at the general store, a thumbs up from a marina somewhere, with boats behind him. In a couple more, he was crouched with one arm around a dog.

Meg stiffened.

It was a brindled pit bull, wearing the same pink camo collar as the one she had seen on her first day there. She hit the back button on the browser and clicked the next name.

A thirty-one-year-old travel influencer who had never posted her planned photo shoot. In one of her selfies, there was a smiling black lab with a rhinestone collar—Meg had seen this one too, sniffing a lamppost.

Her heart racing, Meg picked up her phone and tried to decide what she would say to the police.

A naked woman who looked exactly like her had invited herself inside last night. She had killed a deer—maybe—and eaten some of it. Was that part even illegal? Probably not. She had left a blood-stained hacky sack on Meg's doorstep. And . . .

And Meg had found two websites about missing persons and portals and copycat serial killers and 5G radiation—and she wondered if the woman who looked like her was somehow linked to these things.

Meg put the phone in her pocket without dialing. She decided to pay a visit to Elbow instead. She needed some fresh air. She needed *something*.

The cold water'll knock the crazy right out of you.

Meg grabbed a pocketknife from the junk drawer in the kitchen and stuffed it in her purse, just in case.

The RV Park was eerily quiet, aside from the never-ending roar of waves in the distance. There were no gulls about today, fighting over trash. Meg knocked on the door of Elbow's old camper van and listened for signs of life inside. Nothing. There were dingy curtains covering the windows, and all she could see when she peered through the front were energy bar wrappers and a strange map on the passenger seat. A topographic map, overlaid with psychedelic swirls of neon pink, cherry red, orange, chartreuse, and cyan.

A *magnetic anomaly* map, like the one on the *PERIL NORMAL* blog.

Elbow must have been a part of the "crew" the writer had put together. When he borrowed Meg's phone, she now remembered, he had said something about no one else being here. Had the rest of the crew gone missing before he arrived?

Had Elbow gone missing now too?

Meg walked around the van to peek through the back curtains, but they were drawn tight. She was about to walk away when she saw it. A sticker on the back bumper that read:

I CAN HACK IT!

as long as it's a sack

Meg staggered away, picking up her pace with every step to put distance between herself and the van, as if it was cursed—but she didn't know where she was going. She had hoped to confide in Elbow. The most likely person, surely, to help her untangle this . . . nonsense. Her feet were unsteady beneath her now and a cold sweat was beading up on her forehead. She found the nearest picnic bench and started the breathing exercises she learned before quitting therapy.

Who else could she go to now?

Irina? As off-putting as she was, and as useless as the "witch bottle" had been, she might know what to do now. Or be eccentric enough to believe her, at least.

Pepperwood Lane was one of the half-paved roads to nowhere, and Irina's house was easy to spot before Meg could even read the number on it. The front gate was flanked by twin Buddha statues and the cement steppingstones were carved with Celtic spirals. A rusted Kokopelli played a flute from the top of a garden stake, and faded Tibetan prayer flags twisted in the breeze that had encroached on the morning's stillness. Strange mobiles of mirror fragments swayed from bare fruit tree branches, casting disco ball flickers of light on shingle siding.

And her front door had that same insect-eye mirror design as the one at the general store. Meg lifted the antique bronze door knocker—a crescent moon hanging from an anthropomorphic sun—and rapped it loudly three times. Nothing. She knocked some more until she was convinced there could be no one home.

There was one more person in town who might understand what she was going through.

By the time she got to the long row of beach houses on the cliff, the clouds that had gathered over the ocean behind them were almost the color of soot, lit up occasionally by flashes of lightning in the distance. The wind had picked up, tangling metal and bamboo windchimes into maniacal jazz improvisations.

The artist was outside his rental, loading his easel into the trunk of a white hatchback. There were suitcases at his feet, and his golden retriever was whining and pacing.

"Excuse me," Meg said, and the artist jumped at the sound of her voice, hitting his head on the hatch.

He turned around to face her, wincing. "Yes? I'm in a bit of a hurry here. Trying to beat the storm—"

A crack of thunder punctuated the sentence for him, and he gestured impatiently in the direction it had come from, over the water.

"I saw a man on the beach," Meg blurted, "one who looked exactly like you, while you were at the store."

The artist bent to pick up a suitcase instead of meeting her gaze. "I don't know what you're talking about."

"There's a woman who looks like me," Meg said, and the painter froze. "She showed up at my house last night. I think she killed a deer."

The artist regained his composure, heaved the suitcase roughly into his trunk, and took a crumpled pack of cigarettes out of his coat pocket. He lit one and took a drag before responding to her. "Let me guess. Our mutual friend Irina told you to make a witch bottle?"

"Yes. For protection."

The artist snorted and leaned against the side of the car, watching the wind steal smoke from the cigarette in his fingers. "I think that's how it changes form. Gets your *DNA*. What you really need, I think, is those mirror things. Irina has one. The store. The police department. Some of the nicer houses. Too late now, though."

The golden retriever nudged his wet nose into Meg's palm, piercing the numbness that had surged through her limbs. She looked down at the dog and petted him weakly behind the ears.

"It doesn't like dogs," the artist said. "Doesn't like the taste of them, I guess."

A flash of lightning tore through the clouds in the distance, unzipping the sky to reveal a blinding neon world beyond it. And then it was gone.

"What do you mean it's 'too late?'" Meg's voice came out so small and hoarse that it barely registered over the wind. "*You're* fine."

The artist lifted the final suitcase at his feet and shoved it into his trunk. "I'm fine because it's your problem now." He pushed the hatch down and opened the passenger door to let the dog jump in. "On the next full moon, if all goes well for you, it will be someone else's."

Meg was only halfway home when the sky exploded into a deluge, pelting her and everything else in its path as if it had been holding its bladder too long. Water gushed down the steep road to her house, eating away chunks of dirt on either side of it. Frigid water squished between her toes, and she wished she'd thought to put on boots instead of running shoes. *Be prepared and stay alert for changing conditions.* The earlier warmth of the morning had been washed away by the incoming storm, and by the time she got home she was shivering in violent heaves.

She almost didn't notice the package on her doorstep, with no address or stamp.

Meg brought it inside, set it next to Jeff, and grabbed a towel from the heated rack in the bathroom. She turned on the living room heater, peeled off her sodden clothing, and dried herself as much as she could before curiosity got the best of her dread.

In the mysterious box was another stoneware jug, with a red ribbon tied around its neck. A note attached to the ribbon read:

I've left town for the holidays.
Please give this to the Garcias before the next full moon.
-Irina

When Meg was a child, excited to have her first email address, she received a letter with the subject *DO NOT DELETE*. She happily opened it to find:

I'm very sorry to do this, but this email is cursed. Now you have to send it to 12 friends, or you'll die before the end of the week. I personally know 5 people who ignored this email, and they all died in HORRIBLE ways within days of deleting it. One of them had a plane crash right into their house while they were sleeping. One was struck by lightning, twice. Another had their shoelace sucked into an escalator and cracked their head open when they tripped. You have one hour. DO NOT IGNORE THIS, I AM BEGGING YOU.

Meg had tearfully shown the email to her mother, then threw a screaming fit when her mother promptly deleted it. All that week, she watched her back. She faked being sick to avoid leaving the house for as long as possible. The week passed uneventfully, but she wondered then if the curse would catch up to her later.

Meg put on a warm change of clothes, quickly blow-dried her hair, and packed everything she cared about in her trunk. She turned off the heater and lights, took Jeff with her, and locked up the remains of her new life.

The rain was pouring down even harder now, something Meg didn't think was possible. By the time she reached the car with Jeff, his soggy box was caving in on one side. She put him on the passenger seat.

Even with her wipers at the highest speed, Meg had trouble seeing through the sheets of rain battering her windshield. Sequoia Point Road was a blur of gray and green, split by a yellow line that kept vanishing and reappearing. Meg slowed the car to a crawl, worming her way between cliffsides and towering trees.

She rounded a bend and slammed on her brakes just as a herd of deer leapt into the road in front of her, smears of brown and bone-white racing past her windshield. The car skidded out and she eased off the gas, making sure to brake gently as she'd been taught in defensive driving school. It came to a stop just before hitting the guardrail.

Meg put her head down on the steering wheel. She tried to slow her breathing as the rain slowed to a patter on her roof, but a deep rumbling sound made her look up just in time to see the cliffside collapse.

At the edge of the next bend, a vast gray flow of mud and rocks dragged trees and shrubs with it down the cliff. It all gooped over the roadway, swallowing the guardrail, then that whole section of road abruptly gave way, pushing up the pavement in front of Meg into broken tents of asphalt.

The only road out of Sequoia Point, back to civilization, was now a waterfall.

Meg managed to peel her right hand off the steering wheel it had become glued to. The rain slowed to a trickle on her windshield—now was her chance. She put the car in reverse, wound along the cliffside backwards till she reached a turnout, and drove as fast as the road would allow. Back to whatever awaited her in town.

In her driveway, after turning off the ignition, Meg looked at the collapsed cardboard box in the passenger seat and finally broke down sobbing.

Jeff had surfed Teahupo'o in Tahiti, Shipstern Bluff in Tasmania, the shark-infested waters of Western Australia. He'd gone diving in Egypt's notorious Blue Hole and Tulum's Temple of Doom. Ice climbing at Nanga Parbat in Pakistan. Zip lining in Kathmandu. Heli-skiing, bungee jumping, skydiving.

And he had died just blocks away from their house in the suburbs, on his way to get groceries, in a station wagon. He had been killed in a "low speed collision," when an elderly man ran a stop sign. Jeff was wearing a seat belt. He had been following traffic laws. The air bag that was supposed to protect him had been faulty, and its inflator exploded like a grenade on impact. Shrapnel lodged itself in his brain.

Most accidents happen within five miles of your home, Meg had learned then. Where people feel safe. Where they least expect it.

Inside, Meg gently placed Jeff's disintegrating box on the coffee table and finished the bottle of bourbon.

The next morning, there was a break in the rain. Meg didn't know how long it would last, because her cell phone was no longer getting a signal and her internet appeared to be down. So, she drove to the general store instead of walking.

There were cars and trucks parked in front of the brewery, and two men standing outside having a smoke. They were both wearing white chef's uniforms, one with the sleeves pushed up to reveal heavy tattoos. They nodded hello before going back to their conversation. Such a small thing, but the mundane interaction nearly made Meg cry with relief.

"What's going on at the brewery?" she asked the store clerk, after filling a basket with as many cans of soup and boxes of cereal as it would hold.

"Prepping to reopen after the holiday," the clerk said gruffly. "Good thing they all got here yesterday, or they'd miss out on their holiday bonus. Road's collapsed."

"What about internet? Do you have it here?" Meg asked.

"The phone and cable lines got knocked down by the storm," the clerk said. "Happens almost every winter, sometimes in spring. If the government wasn't so corrupt in this state, they'd have undergrounded the lines by now."

Meg showed him her phone. "My cell's not getting a signal either."

"Mine neither," he said. "Wind must have taken out a cell tower too—wouldn't be the first time."

Meg paid for her canned goods and piled them into her reusable tote, then looked up at the wall of liquor and cigarettes behind the clerk—out of the reach of bored teenage hands. "A bottle of your most expensive vodka too. In case I get snowed in or something."

"Oh, we *rarely* get snow on the coast."

"Noted."

"Count your blessings," the clerk called after her as she left, like he was scolding a sullen child. "At least we've still got electricity."

As Meg packed the tote in her trunk, she saw that the Garcia girl, Emma, had joined the two men smoking outside the brewery. She was wearing a pink wig today, and one of the men was lighting a cigarette for her. When

Emma saw Meg, she thanked the man with an exaggerated curtsy and jogged over to her.

"Please don't tell my parents," she said, flicking ash onto the pavement, and Meg saw now that she looked even paler than she had the other day. "They're not reasonable people."

"Your secret's safe," Meg said. "Just be careful around here, okay? Don't go out alone at night."

"And miss out on this *thriving* nightlife scene?" Emma gestured broadly at the RV park and airstrip. She turned back to Meg and looked her up and down with a hint of suspicion. "So, what do you do, to afford a house here? Are you in finance or real estate, like my parents and everyone else—or something more exciting?"

"Is a life insurance payout exciting?"

"It depends," Emma said. "Did you murder someone to get it? I won't tell. Then we'll be even."

"No, sorry to disappoint." Meg was surprised by how much easier it was to talk to this girl than it had been to talk to everyone who felt *so, so* sorry for her. "My husband was in a car accident."

Jeff had taken out the policy without telling her. There had also been the multimillion-dollar settlement from the airbag manufacturer, but that was more than Meg wanted to get into.

"I'm dying too," the girl said, like she was trying to cheer Meg up with a relatable anecdote. "The chemo didn't do fuck all, but my parents are in denial. They brought me here to get some *fresh sea air* like I'm a heroine in an old book, dying of hysteria or some shit."

The two of them stood in silence for a while, Emma smoking her cigarette and Meg watching gulls circle the cliffs, neither of them saying I'm sorry.

Meg nearly tripped over the antler on her doormat when she brought the groceries inside. She checked behind the potting shed later, holding her sweater over her nose. She had expected to find a rotting body with one antler missing, buzzing with flies. But there were only a few wet tufts of fur in the dirt.

The next day, she found a gull's wing on the doormat, stripped to its delicate bones.

And the next, a tattooed finger with dark hair between its knuckles. She tried to convince herself it belonged to a bad man. Made up a whole backstory for him. He was a cannabis cartel hitman who had killed a rival gang leader's child, and the rival gang had taken their revenge. But they had dropped off his finger on the wrong doorstep.

Another day, Meg stepped outside to find an enormous black paw—so, there were bears here after all. And on Christmas, she found a white chef's hat, splattered red. She buried it behind the shed, along with all the other unwanted gifts.

Sometimes she'd catch a glimpse of her own naked body in the morning mist, a ghostly thing that felt somehow more tangible than she was, running off into the woods.

Fresh missing person posters got pinned to the corkboard in the general store—a line cook, a barback, a man who goes by Elbow. The clerk blamed "sneaker waves."

"Never turn your back on the sea here," he told her. "Folks get swept out every year."

The day before the next full moon, Meg found a pierced ear on her doormat. It was wearing a little silver crescent moon stud, like a child would wear—or someone who can't wear dangly earrings at their waitress job.

Meg took the stoneware jar out of the cupboard she had shoved it into, and tore Irina's note off the red ribbon around its neck.

She had to do it. Emma Garcia was dying. The thing had copied Meg's form, right down to her terrible bangs—surely it would replicate the cancer too? And that would break the chain.

The thing had to die.

Ronaldo Garcia opened the front door, dressed in plaid pajamas and slippers. "Hello, uh—sorry, I'm terrible with names—come in! We were just putting on another pot of coffee."

"Oh, I can't stay," Meg said. "I just brought a late holiday gift for Emma."

"Ooh, what is it?" Louise asked, joining her husband. "Emma's still in bed."

"Uh, it's a—"

Louise pulled the gift bag open with one perfectly manicured nail so she could peer inside. "Oh! One of those witch jar things! Emma *loves* this kind of weird stuff, doesn't she hon?" She turned to her husband.

"Whatever morbid shit makes our baby happy, I always say."

Meg was restless, sitting at home alone that day, wondering if Emma would follow the instructions. Wondering if she had done the right thing. The girl would spend what little time she had left being traumatized. Thinking she was losing her mind. Finding human remains on her doorstep.

How exciting was too exciting? How morbid was too morbid?

Meg tried to keep herself busy by finally tidying up her house. She had let empty soup cans and wine bottles decorate her kitchen counters, hiding the little tabletop frames that said *GATHER* and *GIVE THANKS*. She started sorting them into bags of recycling, until she got to the empty Jim Beam bottle.

She looked at Jeff's box on the coffee table, which now had a corner of Ziploc bag poking out of it where the cardboard had been turned to pulp.

Meg tore through the kitchen cupboards, looking for a funnel, and found a plastic one behind some mason jars. She stuck the funnel in the Jim Beam bottle neck, carefully opened the bag of Jeff's cremains, and poured them into it. She found the little box with Jeff's wedding ring in it, which she'd paired with a lock of his enviably silken hair.

She needed nails. She found an old hammer in the potting shed and used it to pry out three rusty ones jutting from the shed's interior walls.

And wax. She used a "beach memories" scented candle to seal around the bottle cap, after adding the nails to Jeff's hair, cremains, and a pinch of salt.

With the hammer, she smashed the bathroom mirror, then collected the pieces. There was jute twine in the potting shed, and super glue in the junk drawer. She did her best to fashion something resembling the sinister mobiles in Irina's garden. When the glue was dry, she put the mobile in her grocery tote with the bourbon bottle that now contained her husband.

Nothing was too exciting or too morbid for Jeff.

Before she could make it to the Garcias' house, Meg spotted Emma's pink wig at the top of the stairway to the beach. When she finally caught up with her, the girl was on the black sands, crouched next to a little stream running from the cliff to the ocean. She had the stoneware jar in her hand.

"Emma, wait!" Meg called to her, but Emma set the jar on its side in the water and released it.

"You know you can put them in a body of water instead of burying them, right?" Emma said, watching the jar get sucked out past the tide line. "This isn't my first witch bottle; I've got one in the garden back home. Giving it to the sea just seemed more romantic, for a consumptive heroine."

Meg watched nervously as the bottle tumbled to and from the beach.

"It doesn't matter, though," Emma said. "I don't think the magic of the Old World really works here. You know?"

"In Sequoia Point?"

"In America." She stood up and brushed the sand from her black wool tights.

"Wait, I have a gift for your parents," Meg said, sheepishly removing the tangled mobile from her tote. "To hang in the little tree near your front door."

"Oh, that's different," Emma said, holding it up and slowly twirling it so it sparkled in the sunlight. "My mother will hate it. It's perfect."

Meg waited for Emma to disappear up the steps, before running to the water line to grab the jar that had washed back up on the shore.

She buried Jeff right next to the staircase, where she knew the high tide line wouldn't reach, and put a piece of driftwood over his sandy grave.

At home, Meg put on long dish gloves. She cut through the wax seal on the witch bottle with a knife, removed the cork, and dumped its contents into the toilet. She wondered too late, after fishing out the nails and flushing, if the lock of hair would clog her septic system.

When she stood up to peel off the gloves, she came face to face with herself, peering through the bathroom window with her soil-smeared hands on the glass. Her double had followed her here. Had followed the bottle.

Meg turned off the light and slammed the bathroom door behind her.

The next morning, the day of the full moon, Meg's cell phone finally had a signal of two bars. She had almost given up looking as the winter days blurred together. There was still no cable internet, but the nearest cell tower on the other side of the road blockage must have been repaired.

The voicemail screen was a list of *MOM, MOM, MOM, MOM,* from top to bottom. She tapped the most recent one.

"Meggie . . . I hope you're not still blaming yourself for the baby. These things just happen sometimes—even when women are doing all the right things. I drank—*and* smoked—for my entire pregnancy with you. Everyone did back then. And I *knew* I was pregnant . . . Give me a call when you've got a signal again out there. Love you."

Meg tapped the call-back icon and it went straight to voicemail. Her mother was always forgetting to charge her phone. "Mom, I'm okay. I've got electricity and food. But I need something from you if anything *does* happen to me . . . I want you to use Jeff's settlement to fund a dog rescue, here in Sequoia Point. I think he would have liked that . . . Sorry I couldn't call you on Christmas. I love you too."

As bleary sunlight slanted through the woods from the west, Meg cut open the stitches of her *Irina's Creations* sleep mask and swept its contents into a neat pile on the kitchen counter. She found a package of blunt papers in the junk drawer and rolled the cannabis, chamomile, and mugwort into two of them. She smoked one and put the other in the breast pocket of her coat for later.

Before sunset, she walked to the beach to check on Jeff, and the world looked more colorful than it had the day before. This part of the coast was extra green in winter from all the rain, but today even the ocean looked like someone had turned up the color saturation from gray to blue.

When Meg got to the foot of the steps, the driftwood was still where she had left it, and there was no sign of digging in the sand. The tide wasn't as high as she'd expected yet, so she was able to follow a trail of half-eaten mystery bones along the beach. It led to the stream where Emma released her witch bottle, the clear water now running red through the sand.

At the base of the cliff, where a delicate waterfall trickled down the rocks, the thing with Meg's face was squatting in the shadows over a dark, bulky form. As Meg watched, pinned in place by revulsion, her double sank its teeth into the sea lion's side—its mouth seeming to melt through fur, blubber, and bone. When her double raised its head again, the hole in the sea lion's side was *steaming*, as if the other Meg had acid for saliva.

This must be why only a few of the missing people's bodies were found, in various states of "eaten," she thought. More than just eaten, mutilated. But the artist had mentioned the police station in his list of places with protective talismans on their doors. The police must be in on whatever was going on, enough to cover it up. How long had the townsfolk been passing "witch bottles" around? And what had made them do it? Had it been an accidental discovery? Someone using Old World magic to protect themselves from the ravenous thing, and having it take their form instead?

The disappearances on the *MURDER HOUND* blog stretched back to the 1960s. And most of them in winter—was it a seasonal thing? A sort of reverse hibernation?

None of that mattered now, though. The only thing that did was getting her double to notice Jeff's remains. Meg waved her hands over her head and shouted. The thing with her face shrank back into the shadows.

Don't run.

Meg ran until she reached the steps, then stopped to look back over her shoulder. The other Meg was following in that uncanny animal lope of hers. Meg kicked the piece of driftwood off Jeff's burial place, then stabbed at the sand with her foot until the bottle neck was exposed. Her double had stopped to watch her from a few yards away, head cocked, overgrown fingernails contorting her hands into Nosferatu claws at her sides. Meg backed away, climbed halfway up the steps, and waited.

The other Meg approached cautiously and dropped to her knees next to Jeff, then dug with her hideously twisted nails. She held the uncovered bottle up to examine it, as if she was appraising how long the bourbon had been barrel-aged. Unhappy with its maturity, she smashed it unceremoniously against a rock.

Meg held her breath, expecting a dramatic transformation from wife to husband's naked form, but her double sniffed the pile of ashes and hair in the sand and walked back to its sea lion catch.

The sun was getting too low in the sky. Meg looked frantically around the beach, panic bursting through the lingering haze of herbs. What would happen if her double was still her double tomorrow, when the moon was waning?

In the black sands, the silvery insides of shells glittered where they had been cracked open by gulls. *Mussel shells.*

Meg waded out up to her knees in the icy water and clenched her stomach against the cold. The tide pools had mostly been devoured by the surf, but a few larger rocks poked above the water. Mollusks jutted from the volcanic rocks like coats of black fur matted into spikes. She found the largest one and twisted, but the slime of the sea made it slip from her hand, slicing her finger open in the process. She pulled the sleeve of her coat over her fingers and tried again, this time breaking it free from its colony.

After Meg collected six more and filled her pockets with them, she headed back to the beach, bracing herself against the dry parts of the rocks while slipping and tripping her way through buried tide pools. By the time she got to the black sands, she was soaked up to her hips.

Her double looked up from the remains of its sea lion meal and watched her as she approached. Meg crouched a few yards away, took out the pocketknife she'd taken to carrying since the day she found the severed finger, and pried open each mussel shell. She held one up to her mouth, mimed chewing and swallowing, and left them all in a pile on the wet sand.

Meg sat on a large piece of driftwood and watched her double tiptoe toward its easy prey. The thing with her face knelt in the sand, picked up a shell, and greedily slurped the viscous muck from within. It drained the globs of life out of one after another, until all the shells were discarded empty in the sand.

The vibrant colors of the late afternoon were beginning to fade back to gray. Meg took out her lighter and the second herb-infused joint, relieved she had thought to put it in her breast pocket, above the water line. She sucked in another puff of acrid smoke and waited.

As the shadows of rocks and driftwood grew longer in the sand and a fire ignited the sky, Meg watched her double begin to twitch. First it scratched at its lips, then it dragged them downward with its fingers into a distorted frown. Soon its shoulders were twitching, and its fingernail claws were digging involuntarily into its palms. Her double turned to look at her, staggered a few steps forward, and fell.

Meg finished the joint and stripped off her clothing. She felt curiously warm now, even with the shadows encroaching on everything.

"I'm sorry," she said, as she stood over the shuddering form of her own body, before dragging it backward into the choppy surf.

Once they were in the water, she hooked her double's flopping arm around her neck to carry it through the waves. She looked for a break where the water was darker, flatter, calmer.

The day Meg met Jeff, she was on spring break with her friends in Florida, trying to motivate herself to brave the surf. She had always enjoyed swimming in pools, growing up in a land-locked state. Meg spotted a relatively peaceful stretch of water between violently breaking waves, so she had chosen to swim there—and been helplessly swept out to sea.

Jeff had been working as a lifeguard for the summer—not because he needed to work, with his parents' sports gear empire, but just for the thrill of it. He swam out with two lifesavers and pulled Meg back to shore diagonally through the waves. After assuring her that people frequently missed the flags in the sand marking rip current hazards, and not to be embarrassed about it, he had asked her out.

Meg winced at the sting of saltwater in the cut on her finger, while she dragged her double along the beach through chest-high surf. When she reached the swifter, flatter expanse of water, she released the twitching thing like a paper lantern into a creek.

The forceful drag of the current seemed to give her double a last shot of adrenaline, and it thrashed its arms awkwardly, pulling gobs of seaweed out of the surf and getting tangled up in them. Its milky eyes were wide with desperation.

Meg couldn't stand to watch anymore. The warmth of the herbs was beginning to wear off, and so was the strange distance from herself they had given. She turned away and tried to swim back toward the beach, but she hadn't made it far when the thrashing behind her stopped.

Meg spun around and didn't spot her double at first, because it had already been carried so far away. Its head was just a dot bobbing on the water, disappearing, and breaching again. Helpless. Not some unimaginable evil, but an animal like any other, desperate to survive.

Meg dove under the waves, careful to stay out of the rip current. She knew it would be weaker further from the shore, if she could just swim far enough, fast enough. She tried not to think about what else might be in the murky surf with her, drawn to the blood from her finger.

By the time Meg got to the calmer waters where she could cut across, her double was choking frantically and its lips were a sickly blue. As Meg grabbed it and held its head up out of the water, the double's entire body began to seize.

Meg pulled the other Meg out of the current, hoping the waves would help push them back to shore, but her double was gasping as if its lungs required water now instead of air.

Before they could reach the beach, it went limp in Meg's arms, becoming alarmingly still and heavy.

As the last glints of sunlight were devoured by the horizon, the thing that looked like Meg *glowed* from within, burning her skin where their bodies touched. Meg kicked away and watched in awe as her double slipped under the sea and seemed to melt. Its glowing remains floated to the surface, surrounding Meg—both beautiful and unnerving, like the phosphorescent thing the artist had been painting on the beach.

Meg tried to brush the algae-like substance off her skin, but it clung to her arms. She plunged under the water to rinse it off, twisted her body away from it, and swam toward the shore. When she came up for air, she was still surrounded by a neon glow on the water. It was moving with her, in a way that reminded her chillingly of magnetic shavings.

Meg's finger was beginning to itch unbearably. She looked down to see the bioluminescence gathering around her cut, clinging to it. *Vanishing into it.* She tried to shake it off, tried to swim faster—but before she could make it to dry land, the glowing substance had all seeped inside her, burning through her veins.

She could already feel it. The hunger. A swirling pit had opened in her stomach, aching to be fed. A memory of the taste of blood singed her tongue—metallic, like the rusty nail she had put in her mouth as a child. She had sucked the blood from a cut on her arm once too, just to see what it tasted like, and spat it out. The disgust in the memory was gone now, replaced by a tormented longing.

Meg couldn't go back to the shore. She couldn't let the thing inside her feed. She had to turn around, swim back into the rip current, and keep going toward the horizon until she couldn't go any further.

Before she could force her legs into motion, though, she saw the most magnificent thing. All along the beach, glittering rifts began to form, like the gold seams she had seen used to repair cracked pottery in a Japanese museum. Most of these rifts were tiny, smaller than her hand. But out of the corner of her eye, something gleamed like a golden dome on a Russian cathedral.

It was the guano covered island of rock looming over the sea. A glowing rift tore through it from top to bottom, extending under the water and lighting it up like a swimming pool.

A *portal*.

If the thing inside her had come out of it, and it could survive here—maybe Meg could survive on the other side. An entirely new world to explore, the likes of which even Jeff had never seen on his deepest dives. It couldn't be worse than the guarantee of drowning, if she swam into the rip current. Her limbs were already heavy, and her muscles burned with exertion as she fought to keep her head above the waves.

Meg swam toward the light glimmering in the water. But the closer she got, the more she was overcome with dread—not her own dread this time, but a fear that came from the same place as her new hunger.

The thing didn't want to return to the portal. It cowered inside her, urging her to go back to the beach.

It wasn't an apex predator, she realized then. Not over there, where it came from. There was something larger, stronger, worse.

Meg treaded water. This wasn't who she was.

She wanted to live. Had always wanted it. Had never understood why Jeff courted death, harder than he could ever court her. She wished now that she had yelled at him every time he told her to "live a little." Living didn't have to be the path of most resistance, a war declared against death, always pushing the front lines. It could be a home with a fireplace and a lazy old dog curled at her feet. It could be reading a mystery she knew would be solved by the end of the book.

As she let the waves wash her back to shore, the hunger grew more insistent, impossible to resist. But Meg was a literate animal. She had access to the internet. They didn't have to blindly choose their victims, the way the creature had before it was part of her. There were terrible people out there, doing terrible things without remorse. Psychopaths. Defilers of the Earth—this place neither she nor the thing inside her wanted to leave.

Under the waning moon, the golden cracks in the cliffs began to close, but what remained here in the darkness was equally magnificent.

ABOUT THE AUTHORS

JOHN K. PECK is a Berlin-based writer and musician. His writing has appeared in a diverse range of journals including *Interzone, Pyre, voidspace, Cosmic Horror Monthly, Cold Signal, McSweeney's, Glasgow Review of Books,* and Lost in Cult's *The Horror: Mansion.* He is also the editor of *Degraded Orbit,* a website dedicated to unusual architecture, abandoned places, and underground writing and art.
www.johnkpeck.com

L. MAHLER is a designer and doctoral researcher specializing in cellulose-based origami structures and living design systems. Her academic writing has been published in various journals and conference proceedings, and her design works were recently featured at Dutch Design Week and Naturkundemuseum Bayern. She splits her time between Helsinki and Berlin, where her free hours are spent visiting the sauna and foraging for bast fibers.

ÍDE HENNESSY (she/they) lives in Humboldt County, California with her partner and three special needs cats who can see ghosts. Her fiction has appeared in *Strange Horizons, Reckoning, Cosmic Horror Monthly,* Dark Matter's *The Off-Season: Coastal New Weird* anthology, *Fusion Fragment, Flash Point SF, King Ludd's Rag,* and more. She also writes lyrics for and performs with darkwave band Control Voltage. You can find her at idehennessy.com, on Bluesky as ideofmarch, and on Instagram and Twitter as ahennessyvsop.

ABOUT THE ARTISTS

Viviana is a Portuguese artist most known as **ECHO ECHO**. Her creative influence is born in observing nature to the smallest details and recreating that feeling in her illustrations. She likes to create new worlds, bringing some sort of reality to these fantasy worlds while filling them with psychedelic manifestations of her imagination. Find more of her work on Instagram @echoechoillustrations.

EVANGELINE GALLAGHER is an award-winning illustrator from Baltimore, Maryland. They received their BFA in Illustration from the Maryland Institute College of Art in 2018. When they aren't drawing they're probably hanging out with their dog, Charlie, or losing at a board game. They possess the speed and enthusiasm of 10,000 illustrators.

CONTENT WARNINGS

Being a work of mature Horror, a degree of violence, gore, and/or death is to be expected.

In addition, **SEQUOIA POINT** contains scenes of:

- **Miscarriage (off-page)**

- **Dead wildlife**

- **Alcoholism**

- **Depression**

Please be advised.

More information at
www.tenebrouspress.com

GRAB ANOTHER
TENEBROUS TITLE!

GRAB ANOTHER TENEBROUS TITLE!

TENEBROUS PRESS

aims to drag the malleable Horror genre into newer, Weirder territory with stories that are incisive, provocative, intelligent and terrifying; delivered by voices diverse and unsung.

FIND OUT MORE:

www.tenebrouspress.com
Social Media @TenebrousPress

NEW WEIRD HORROR

TENEBROUS

10p

PRESS

www.ingramcontent.com/pod-product-compliance
Lightning Source LLC
Chambersburg PA
CBHW020440060225
21439CB00004B/11